3/09

EssexWorks.

For a better quality of life

FTN/C

Please return this book on or before the date shown above. To renew go to www.essex.gov.uk/libraries, ring 0845 603 7628 or go to any Essex library.

SPACE
X

Essex County Council

D0261253

'How about,' Leandro suggested, 'we escape? Go and find some proper food.' He looked pointedly at her barely touched glass. 'And wine you can actually drink.'

He had a voice like melted chocolate, and eyes to match. Olive skin betraying his Mediterranean ancestry. Dark hair that was cut short, but Becky would just bet turned curly if he were in a rainstorm; it made her itch to slide her fingers into it.

And he had the sexiest mouth she'd ever, ever seen.

Leandro Herrera was a complete stranger. She knew nothing about him. She really ought to refuse. Politely, but refuse.

'Yes. I'd love to.'

'Good.' He stood up again and held a hand out to her, and she let him draw her to her feet. Even though she was five foot seven in heels, he was a good six inches taller than she was. Broad-shouldered. Strong.

He could have made her feel intimidated.

Instead, he made her feel safe. And she couldn't remember when she'd last felt like this…

Kate Hardy lives in Norwich, in the east of England, with her husband, two young children, one bouncy spaniel, and too many books to count! When she's not busy writing romance or researching local history, she helps out at her children's schools; she's a school governor and chair of the PTA. She also loves cooking—spot the recipes sneaked into her books! (They're also on her website, along with extracts and stories behind the books.) Writing for Mills & Boon has been a dream come true for Kate—something she wanted to do ever since she was twelve. She's been writing Medical™ Romances for nearly five years now, and also writes for Modern Heat. She says it's the best of both worlds, because she gets to learn lots of new things when she's researching the background to a book: add a touch of passion, drama and danger, a new gorgeous hero every time, and it's the perfect job!

Kate's always delighted to hear from readers, so do drop in to her website at www.katehardy.com

Recent titles by the same author:

In Medical™ Romance
THE DOCTOR'S ROYAL LOVE-CHILD
  (Brides of Penhally Bay)
THE ITALIAN GP'S BRIDE
THE CONSULTANT'S NEW-FOUND FAMILY

In Modern Heat
SOLD TO THE HIGHEST BIDDER!
BREAKFAST AT GIOVANNI'S

THE SPANISH DOCTOR'S LOVE-CHILD

BY
KATE HARDY

MILLS & BOON®
Pure reading pleasure™

All the characters in this book have no existence outside
the imagination of the author, and have no relation
whatsoever to anyone bearing the same name or names.
They are not even distantly inspired by any individual
known or unknown to the author, and all the incidents
are pure invention.

First published in Great Britain 2008
Large Print edition 2009
Harlequin Mills & Boon Limited,
Eton House, 18-24 Paradise Road,
Richmond, Surrey TW9 1SR

© Kate Hardy 2008

ISBN: 978 0 263 20491 9

Set in Times Roman 16½ on 19 pt.
17-0209-51820

Printed and bound in Great Britain
by CPI Antony Rowe, Chippenham, Wiltshire

For Terri and Lee, with much love

CHAPTER ONE

'ROD HAWES, fifty-four, had just got a strike at tenpin bowling when he started having chest pains,' Ed, the paramedic, told Becky and David as he wheeled the trolley into Resus. 'His wife and kids are on their way.'

Becky glanced at their patient, not liking his colour or the sheen of sweat on his skin.

'He described the pain as being like an elephant sitting on his chest,' Ed continued.

Classic symptoms. So she was expecting the paramedic's next comment: 'The pain wasn't relieved by GTN and from the trace we think he's had an MI. We've cannulated and given him oxygen, but no aspirin because he's got a stomach ulcer.'

A complication they could really do without.

Almost before David asked, she had a syringe in her hand and bottles. 'Usual bloods?' she asked.

He nodded. 'Has he had an antiemetic?' David asked the paramedic.

'Not yet.'

'I'm on it,' Becky said, swiftly sorting out the bloods. She'd administered an antiemetic through the cannula and set up the electrocardiograph leads to take a trace of the heart's activity by the time David had finished taking the patient's history.

Strange how everything slowed right down in the middle of an emergency. Their patient's life was at stake, but the team had worked together for so long that they all knew exactly what to do. Everything slotted together in the right place and at the right time.

And it was a shame that today was going to be the last time they'd work together. David was flying out to Africa almost straight after his shift to do a six-month stint with Doctors Without Borders.

Becky only hoped that the new consultant would be as thorough and as genuinely nice as David, treating the patients and staff alike with respect and kindness. Human Resources hadn't exactly been generous with their information, and even the hospital grapevine had drawn a blank. All they knew about the new consultant was that he was male.

They were about to administer thrombolytic drugs when she saw the pattern on the ECG change. 'He's gone into VT.'

Hardly surprising. Becky knew that most patients who'd had a heart attack developed an abnormal heart rhythm afterwards. VT, or ventricular tachycardia, was where a ventricle, one of the lower chambers of the heart, beat too fast; it could lead to ventricular fibrillation, where the heart contracted but didn't pump blood around the body, and it was life-threatening.

'OK. We know the drill,' David said wryly. 'Crash team. Mina, can you remove the clothing from Rod's upper body, so we can position the paddles more easily?' he asked the first-year foundation doctor.

Mina did so while David checked Rod's intubation and Becky checked his pulse. 'He's in pulseless VT,' she reported.

David sighed and put one paddle on the apex position and the other on the right of Rod's breastbone, just below the clavicle. 'Charging to two hundred,' he said. 'Stand clear.'

Everyone took their hands off the patient.

'Shocking now.'

Becky glanced at the ECG. 'No response. He's still in VT.'

They waited ten seconds to see if the ECG trace changed—the protocol was that you didn't check the pulse after a shock unless the heart rhythm changed.

'Charging to two hundred again,' David said, keeping the paddles on the gel pads. 'And clear. Shocking now.'

Still no response.

'Charging to three-sixty,' David said, 'and clear. Shocking now.'

To everyone's relief, the ECG showed a clear sinus rhythm—the normal beat of the heart.

Becky checked Rod's pulse and her stomach plummeted. 'No pulse. He's gone into PEA.' PEA, or pulseless electrical activity, was where the heart rhythm seemed normal on the ECG screen, showing that there was electrical activity within the heart, but the heart wasn't actually pumping blood around the patient's body.

He was intubated, on oxygen, and there was no sign of a bleed; they also knew from the history that the patient had given them that he wasn't on any medication and hadn't taken any drugs. So that narrowed down the likely causes of the problem.

David grimaced. 'My money's on thrombosis—a huge MI.'

Which meant the chances of a good result were slim. Becky knew that when a patient had gone into PEA, if they couldn't find the underlying cause fast enough, they treated the patient as if they were in cardiac arrest. The odds weren't on their side, but she drew up a milligram of epinephrine and handed it to David. 'Want me to bag while you do the compressions?'

He nodded. 'Sure I can't persuade you to come with me? We could do with a really good nurse on the team. Especially one who's a nurse practitioner.'

'Thanks, but I'm happy here in Manchester,' she said. Maybe a year or eighteen months ago, she would've jumped at the chance to get away from the mess of her failed marriage—

and the even messier bit she'd never told anyone about, even her closest friends—but she'd stuck it out and her life was back on an even keel now.

'Hmm.' David looked at the ECG monitor. 'As the underlying rhythm's bradycardia, let's try atropine as well.'

She drew up a milligram and checked it, then David administered the drug.

Just respond, she begged their patient silently. *You've got a family on its way to you, needing you to wake up.* Rod Hawes was a family man who'd been out with his wife and kids, having fun. Why the hell did this sort of thing have to happen? Why couldn't it happen instead to someone who'd made his family's life miserable and wouldn't be missed?

She pushed the thought away. Not here. Not now. Despite the two rotten days she'd just spent in London, this wasn't the time or place to think about that. She needed to stay detached, do her job.

Ten sequences of basic life support over three minutes, checking for a pulse after each one.

'Still no pulse,' she reported.

'No change on the ECG,' Mina said.

Another milligram of epinephrine. She counted the rhythm: fifteen chest compressions to two breaths.

Still nothing.

Come on, come on, she thought. *Go into VF so we can go back to shocking you. Get your heart started again.*

Irene, one of the staff nurses, came in. 'His family's here,' she said.

David nodded, his face grim. 'Now's not a good time for them to see him. Can you take them to the relatives' room and look after them? I'll be with them as soon as I can. As soon as we get him to respond.'

'Will do.'

But after they'd been working for twenty minutes, David stopped. 'It's not going to happen,' he said softly. 'His brain's been without oxygen for twenty minutes. He's gone. Everyone agreed that we call it?'

One by one, very quietly, the rest of the team agreed.

'Right. Time of death...' he looked at the clock '...four forty-seven. Thanks for your help, team. Sorry we didn't make it.' He raked a hand through his hair. 'This sucks. Big time.' He sighed. 'Better go see his family.'

'Do you want me to do it?' Becky asked.

He patted her shoulder. 'You're a sweetheart for offering—but it's my responsibility. I'll do it.'

'I'll call his GP, then, and inform the coroner,' she said. 'And fill out the forms for you to sign.'

'Let's hope I'm a bit better than this when I get out to Africa,' he said, shaking his head in apparent disgust with himself.

'Hey. Don't beat yourself up. You know as well as I do that PEA doesn't have a good prognosis—and one in three patients with an MI don't even make it to the emergency department in the first place. You did your best. We all did.'

Neither of them said it, but she knew they were both thinking it: their best just hadn't been good enough.

And although Becky was based in the minor injuries section for the rest of her shift and concentrated on treating each patient, there was still that underlying misery she felt whenever they lost a patient. A dull, heavy feeling that wouldn't shift, even by the time she got home.

'Bad day?' Tanya, her housemate, asked as she walked in.

'Does it show?'

Tanya nodded. 'From the look on your face, I'd say you lost a patient.'

'Yes.'

Tanya gave her a sympathetic hug. 'That's exactly why I could never work in emergency medicine. At least in paediatrics most of our patients make it.'

'We don't lose *that* many,' Becky protested.

'You know what I mean.' Tanya switched the kettle on. 'You need tea. Actually, I've got a better idea than that. You know the newbie doctors on our ward?'

'The first-year foundation doctors have been in for two months now. They're not exactly newbies any more,' Becky said.

Tanya grinned. 'If you ask me, they're still a bit wet behind the ears! But Joe's pretty cute. And he's having a party tonight. Why don't you come with me?'

'I wasn't invited,' Becky pointed out.

'He said I could bring a friend.' Tanya brushed her objection aside. 'What you need is a good night out. Lots of loud music, maybe a bit too much red wine, and let your hair down.'

'Down.' Becky flicked the ends of her short hair. 'And that would be how, exactly, Tan?'

Tanya laughed. 'Oh, you. Seriously, come with me. It'll be a laugh.'

After the week she'd had—including two days spent being the dutiful granddaughter and resenting every second of it—Becky could really do with a laugh. 'OK. Thanks. I will.'

Lord, he needed a breather from this party, Leandro thought.

Given the choice between spending his first Saturday in Manchester completely on his own in a rented flat, wondering why the hell he'd left Barcelona, and coming to a party where he was likely to meet some of his new colleagues, Leandro had accepted the invitation with a smile. Enthusiasm, even.

But he'd forgotten what kind of parties junior doctors threw.

Ones with plenty of cheap wine, barely edible snacks that left you hungry, and terrible music played at the kind of volume where conversations had to be conducted at shouting pitch. Where there was barely any room to move, because so many people were packed into the place.

Thirty-five years old, and he'd hit middle age, he thought ruefully. Because he was beginning to wish he'd stayed in after all.

Leandro took a swig from the bottle of beer and wandered into the garden, thinking at least he'd find a quiet corner there. Although it was April, it was warm enough for him not to need a coat.

And then he saw her.

Sitting on a bench tucked away in a quiet corner of the garden, with her shoes off and her knees drawn up to her chin, looking as though she wanted to be a hundred miles away, too. A kindred spirit, perhaps?

He walked over to the bench. 'Do you mind if I join you?'

She looked up at him and frowned. 'Sorry. I didn't catch what you said.'

Hardly surprising. She'd probably been deafened by the music blasting from inside the house.

'I said, do you mind if I join you?' he repeated, this time a little louder.

She shrugged and uncurled, making room for him to sit beside her. 'Help yourself.'

Even though the sun had set an hour or so ago, the light shining into the garden from the kitchen was bright enough for him to see her properly. She had short brown hair, the sort that would go into spiral curls if she let it grow, and dark blue eyes that looked haunted. And a perfect rosebud of a mouth that sent a frisson of desire down his spine.

'*Gràcies.*' He sat down. 'Leandro Herrera.' He held his free hand out to her. She took it, and the frisson down his spine grew stronger.

'Rebecca Marston. Everyone calls me Becky,' she said, shaking his hand. Her grip was cool, firm, precise—and he liked it.

'Which part of Spain do you come from?' she asked.

'Barcelona.'

She looked thoughtful. 'Catalunya.'

He raised an eyebrow. 'I'm impressed. You know Spain?'

'Not really. I had a penfriend years ago—our teacher had spent a year in Spain and taught at a school there, and she told us a bit about the country. She set up a penfriend scheme between the two schools.' She smiled. 'In the years before email and chat rooms. But those early lessons helped when it came to taking exams.'

'Parla català?' he asked.

She shook her head. 'Sorry. I assume you're asking me if I speak Catalan—I don't, and my Spanish is horribly rusty. But your English is excellent.'

'Gràcies. I learned from an early age.' He inclined his head in acknowledgement. 'So, Rebecca—Becky. Do you always escape into the garden at parties?'

She wrinkled her nose. 'No, though I am at this one. My housemate persuaded me to come with her because she thought it would do me good to…' And then she gave him the most gorgeously mischievous smile, indicating the ends of her short hair. 'To let my hair down a bit.'

He smiled back. 'And you're regretting letting her persuade you?'

She nodded. 'This really isn't my kind of thing.'

'Not mine either,' he admitted. 'And I heard someone say something about karaoke.'

Becky closed her eyes briefly. 'Help. I'm not

sure what's worse—being bullied into singing something in front of a crowd or having to listen to other people singing out of key or out of rhythm.'

'Especially when they've drunk enough to think they're in tune and sound as good as their favourite pop star,' he added dryly. 'I think I'm going to call it a night.'

'I don't blame you.'

Something in her face told him that she felt the same way. And even though he had no intention of seeing her again after tonight, it would be good to have company rather than going back to his flat on his own. Dinner wouldn't hurt. So he gave into the impulse and asked, 'Have you eaten tonight?'

'Just some nibbles here.'

'How about,' he suggested, 'we escape? Go and find some proper food.' He looked pointedly at her barely touched glass. 'And wine you can actually drink.'

He had a voice like melted chocolate, and eyes to match. Olive skin betraying his Mediterranean ancestry. Dark hair that was cut short, but Becky would just bet turned curly if he were in a rainstorm; it made her itch to slide her fingers into it.

And he had the sexiest mouth she'd ever, ever seen.

Leandro Herrera was a complete stranger. She knew nothing about him. He could be some kind of maniac. She really ought to refuse. Politely, but refuse.

And then her grandfather's voice echoed in her head.

I should think so, too. Why you couldn't just settle down and have children and support your husband, I'll never know. Going off with a complete stranger, indeed. No moral fibre, your generation...

Oh, shut *up*, Gramps, Becky thought. She was a grown woman. And in her view strangers were friends you hadn't yet met. If a gorgeous man invited her out to dinner, and she wanted to go, then it was her *choice*. And she was going to do it.

'Yes. I'd love to.'

'Good.' He stood up again and held a hand out to her. She slipped her feet back into her shoes, then took his hand and let him draw her to her feet. Even though she was five feet seven in heels, he was a good six inches taller than she was. Broad shouldered. Strong.

He could've made her feel intimidated.

Instead, he made her feel safe. And she couldn't remember when she'd last felt like this.

Certainly not with Michael, who'd taken every safety net away from her.

'I'd better let my housemate know I'm leaving,' she said.

'Of course. And I need to say goodbye and thank you to my host.'

Old-fashioned good manners. She liked that, too.

'I'll meet you by the front door, yes?' he suggested.

She smiled back. 'Sure.'

The rooms were crowded and the deep bass of the music was enough to give her a headache. She couldn't see her housemate anywhere in the crush. 'Have you seen Tanya?' she asked several of the paediatric nurses who worked with Tanya. At the fifth 'Sorry' she gave up. She walked back into the garden, where it was quiet enough to think straight, and texted her friend. *Being party pooper. C U back home. Have a good time!*

Then she headed back to the kitchen and found Joe. 'Thanks for letting me come with Tanya.'

'No worries. We've got loads of room.' The junior doctor frowned. 'You're not going already, are you?'

'I'm not really in a party mood,' she said ruefully. 'Had a bad shift this afternoon.'

'You're in the emergency department, aren't you?' At her nod, he looked sympathetic—clearly he'd guessed the outcome of her day. 'Well, see you around. Thanks for coming.'

She smiled back. 'Enjoy yourself.'

Joe grinned. 'Oh, I plan to!'

Leandro was waiting for her by the front door. 'Ready?' he asked.

She still had the chance to say no. She could call a taxi and go home on her own.

But there was something about Leandro's smile, the warmth in his eyes, that told her this was a man she could trust. 'Ready,' she said.

CHAPTER TWO

'So do you know anywhere nearby that serves reasonable food?' Leandro asked.

Becky glanced at her watch. 'At this time on a Saturday night, to be honest, most of the places I know are going to be full.'

'Then I have a suggestion—seeing as I'm used to eating late in Spain, and if you don't mind waiting a few minutes more, maybe I can cook us dinner.'

'You're offering to cook for me?' She looked at him in surprise.

He spread his hands. 'What's so strange about that?'

She didn't really know him, and he'd just offered to cook her a meal. Part of her thought that this was a seriously bad idea. Going for dinner with a stranger in a public place where she could call a taxi and escape if she needed to would be one thing; going to his home was just asking for trouble. But, on the other hand, her instincts were rarely wrong—and she didn't have any mental warning bells about Leandro Herrera.

Quite the opposite.

'I… Well. I'm just not used to men who can cook,' she hedged. Her father was incredibly old-fashioned in his outlook and had always maintained the kitchen was her mother's domain—he wouldn't so much as heat up a pizza in the oven. Her grandfather was even worse—he actually expected women to withdraw from the table after dinner and leave the men to port and cigars. Most of the male doctors she knew ate in the hospital canteen and lived on cereals or take-away food at home. And as for Michael…

The less she thought about her ex-husband, the better.

'The first cookbook published in Spain was from Catalonia,' Leandro said with a smile. '*Libre del Coc*. It was nearly five hundred years ago, and my people are very proud of that. My mother taught me to cook.'

He didn't mention his father, she noticed. Or

maybe his father had been more like the men she'd grown up with.

'You need to tell your friend where you're going,' Leandro added. 'So she knows where you are and who you're with and won't have to worry about you.'

He rose a couple more notches in her estimation. That kind of thoughtfulness was rare, in her experience. Or maybe the men in Catalonia had a more developed protective instinct than the men she was used to. 'Thank you.' She pulled her mobile phone out of her bag and tried calling Tanya. 'Ah. No answer.'

'She probably can't hear you above the music,' he said with a wry smile.

'I'll text her,' Becky said, and swiftly tapped in a message. *Having dinner with Leandro Herrera.* He gave her his address, and she felt her eyes widen. He lived in West Didsbury, one of the more upmarket districts of Manchester. She added his address to her text message and sent it to Tanya.

'If we go to the end of the street we'll be on the main road and we'll be able to flag down a taxi, yes?' he asked.

She nodded. 'Have you lived here long?'

'I moved here this week. How about you?'

'Six years.'

'I'm looking forward to exploring the city,' he said. 'So where do you recommend I start?'

'It depends what you like. The theatres are good; there are music venues and clubs to suit all tastes; and the museum's got an amazing collection of pre-Raphaelite art.'

'Not something I know,' he admitted. 'I know more about the Modernistes. Gaudí's from my home city. And obviously we have the Picasso museum in Barcelona.' He raised an eyebrow. 'So you like art.'

She nodded. 'Not that I get much time to visit the galleries in Manchester.' She didn't want him thinking that was a hint, so she changed the subject swiftly. 'There's an off-licence not far from here. Can we go there before we get a taxi?'

'Why?'

'Because if you're cooking dinner, the least I can do is provide the wine.' She smiled. 'I promise it'll be better than that stuff in the box at the party.'

He laughed. 'That wouldn't be difficult. But there's really no need.'

Oh, yes, there was. She didn't want to be beholden to him. She'd had too many years of feeling beholden. 'If I don't contribute, then I don't feel able to accept your offer,' she said quietly.

He sighed. 'In my world, when you ask someone to dinner, you don't expect them to pay the bill.'

'In my world,' she retorted, 'friends share. Which includes the bill. Or, in this case, make a contribution in the form of wine.'

He inclined his head in acknowledgement. 'Then I had better accept your offer. *Gràcies*, Becky.'

They walked in relaxed silence to the parade of shops round the corner. 'Red or white?' Becky asked.

'Either.'

She opted for both: a fruity New Zealand sauvignon blanc and a rioja.

He hailed a taxi, gave the driver his address, and insisted on paying the fare at the other end. 'No arguments, this time,' he told Becky.

His house was a Victorian terrace, set in a leafy, tree-lined road. The kind of house she would've loved—the kind she and Michael had planned to move to. Except his price had been too high, one she just hadn't been prepared to pay. Especially after all the dreams had come crashing down round her. And there was no way she could afford a house on her own, so after the divorce she'd gone back to renting.

'Nice house,' she said as he ushered her inside. The décor didn't give much away—the colour scheme was neutral and there weren't any prints on the wall—but if he'd only just moved in he probably hadn't had time to change it to suit his tastes.

'That's what I thought when I looked around. I need to check with the agency if I can put anything on the walls, but in the meantime I can live with it.'

So it was rented rather than his own. Not that it was so surprising. Even if he planned to buy a house, it would take time to sort out.

'Let me get you a drink. Would you like a glass of wine, or would you prefer coffee for now?'

'I'd love a coffee, actually. Thank you.'

'*De res.*' Her confusion must have been obvious, because he smiled. 'That's "You're welcome".'

She smiled back. 'So you're going to teach me some Catalan?'

'Sure. But let's eat first, yes?'

She followed him into the kitchen.

'Would you rather eat here or in the dining room?' he asked.

'I don't mind.'

'Here, then.' He gestured to the chair and switched the kettle on. 'How do you take your coffee?'

'A little milk, no sugar, please.' And most of the time, at work, it was cold.

'Are you OK with chicken?' he asked.

'Lovely. Anything I can do to help?'

'No, it's fine. Do you mind if I put some music on? I prefer cooking to music.'

'Sure.' Though Becky really, really hoped he didn't like the kind of dance music they'd been playing at the party. She liked the kind of music you could sing along to, something with a tune.

It seemed that Leandro preferred classical—she didn't recognise the soft, gentle guitar piece, but liked what she heard. 'That's pretty. What is it?'

'One of Mozart's divertimenti. One of my favourites for chilling out.'

'So the music at the party really wasn't your sort of thing.'

He smiled ruefully. 'I must be getting old.'

Hardly. She felt the same. 'You don't look older than your early thirties.'

'I'm thirty-five. And I do like contemporary music...just not the stuff they were playing.' He handed her a mug of coffee: just as she liked it, strong with just a splash of milk. So he'd been listening to what she'd said. That, in her experience, made a very pleasant change.

'*Gràcies,*' she said.

He looked pleased that she'd tried to use his own language. '*De res,*' he said, and started preparing their meal. He worked swiftly and accurately, she noticed, slicing and chopping. 'Are you a chef?' she asked.

He laughed. 'No. I just enjoy cooking. It relaxes me—that, and good music.'

He didn't venture any information about what he did for a living, and Becky wasn't in the mood for being pushy. She'd been pushed too hard herself over the last few days, and right now she just wanted to relax and unwind and not have to think about anything at all. She sipped her coffee and enjoyed listening to the music and watching him sizzle chicken in a pan.

'That smells gorgeous,' she said.

'Twenty minutes, and it'll be done.' He rummaged in the fridge, arranged a few things on a plate, and brought it over to the little kitchen table.

'Tapas?' she asked.

He nodded. 'Though strictly speaking it's *tapes* in Catalan. I'm sorry, this is a bit scrappy because I wasn't planning to entertain—just some Manzanilla olives, chorizo and cheese. But it'll keep us going until the chicken is done.' He took two wineglasses from the cupboard. 'Red or white?'

'Either.'

'Red, then.' He opened the bottle of rioja. 'Nice choice,' he said, pouring them both a glass, and sat down opposite her. 'Well. *Salut.*' He raised his glass.

She did likewise. 'Cheers.'

It was easy to relax with Leandro—he kept the conversation light and didn't push past her personal boundaries. By the time he brought over their main course, Becky was thoroughly relaxed.

'This looks gorgeous.'

'*Pollastre romesco*—chicken with romesco sauce. It's a mixture of almonds, tomato, garlic and vinegar. And this is *espinacas a la Catalana*—spinach with raisins and pine nuts,' he added, gesturing to the green vegetable. 'Sorry, I don't have any potatoes. But would you like some bread with your meal?'

'No, this is fine, thanks.' She tasted a mouthful. 'Wow. You're a fantastic cook.'

'Thank you.' He smiled. 'Spanish food and drink isn't just paella and sherry, you know.'

'It sounds as if you're sick of being stereotyped.'

He rolled his eyes. 'So many people think that Spain is all about bullfights and guitars and waiters called Manuel. And there's much more to it than that.'

'Tell me,' she invited. And when he described the buildings and the festivals and the fireworks and the human 'towers' of acrobats reaching up nine storeys, his eyes glittering with enthusiasm for his native city, she could just imagine herself there.

For dessert, Leandro offered her nectarines, and then he made more coffee and brought out a box of chocolates. Really, really good chocolates. Ones she adored but almost never bought for herself because she couldn't justify the indulgence except on her birthday or at Christmas.

'This,' she said, 'is perfect. A million times better than what was on offer at Joe's.'

'So how come you ended up at the party?'

'Joe works with my housemate. Tanya thought the party might cheer me up—it's been the day from hell, and I've also been away for a couple of days.'

'And you wish you were still away?' he asked.

Becky thought of the rows and the silences. The expectations that she never fulfilled. The constant disappointment on her parents' faces because she hadn't settled down and produced grandchildren. Not that they would've been sympathetic if she'd told them what had really happened with Michael—or if she'd told them about the baby she'd lost. They would've blamed her, and she already blamed herself enough. She didn't need the extra guilt. Which was why she'd never told anyone the full story.

'No. I'm glad to be back in Manchester. I only went back to London because I was expected to,' she admitted. 'It was a family birthday, so I had to be there.'

'But you couldn't wait to get away?' He took another chocolate. 'I know *exactly* what you mean.'

Clearly his family was as difficult as her own, though he'd sounded affectionate before when he'd mentioned his mother teaching him to cook.

'So what about you?' she asked. 'How do you know Joe?'

'I don't, really. It was a loose invitation—an acquaintance of an acquaintance, and I thought it was a better option than being on my own my first Saturday night in Manchester.' He shrugged. 'Though I found something better. An evening with good food, good wine, good conversation and good company.'

'Here's to that,' she said, raising her wine-glass. 'And definitely better music.'

'Though this isn't quite what you'd dance to,' he said. 'And you need dancing at a party.' His gaze held hers for a moment. 'Would you like to dance with me?'

'I'm no good at dancing,' she said. 'I have two left feet.'

'Then let me teach you.' He stood up and took her hand. The touch of his skin against hers sent a frisson of desire down her spine, and she let him lead her through to the living room.

'Something to dance to. Now, let me see.' He glanced along the rack of CDs.

The sound system in his living room was seriously expensive, Becky noticed. Given those chocolates, Leandro was a man who clearly liked the best. And expected the best.

So this idea of dancing was a really bad one. Especially as he hadn't listened to her warning that it wasn't her forte.

But then she didn't have the chance to think any more as the music flooded the room: a soft intro, and then a really sexy, haunting voice singing in Spanish. She had no idea what the man was singing about, but she loved his voice. 'Who's this?' she asked.

Leandro named a Spanish singer she'd never heard of. 'He's popular in my country,' he added with a smile. 'Now, the dance.' He took her hands and placed one on his shoulder and the other on his waist. 'This is for balance. Just follow my lead, and you'll be fine.' He smiled at her. 'The rhythm is slow, slow, quick, quick, slow.'

Oh-h-h. She remembered a chick-flick she'd gone to see with a crowd of her female friends. 'Is this the tango?'

He inclined his head. 'It doesn't have to be as showy as the ones you see in films. I'm not going to bend you over backwards or place your cheek next to mine so we're facing the same way and stalk down the room. Just relax, feel the beat of the music and trust me to guide you.'

Before she knew it, they were dancing. It felt as if she were floating. Not stumbling, as she had before.

'Two left feet? I don't think so,' he whispered, holding her close.

Probably because he was an incredible dancer and she was simply following his movements.

She could feel the warmth of his skin through his thin cotton shirt, and she was so aware of the way he was holding her, one hand resting on her shoulder and the other on her waist. Holding her close. Moving as one with her.

'You have beautiful eyes,' he said softly. 'Like

the colour of a sky on a late spring evening, just as the stars are starting to come out.'

Flattery, she knew. But it sent a little flutter through her. 'Thank you.'

They danced in silence a while longer, then she felt his lips brush lightly against her cheek. Just once. And then he paused, clearly waiting for her signal.

She could drop her hands and take a step back. Thank him for the evening, and call a taxi.

Or for once she could live dangerously.

How long had it been since she'd found a man as attractive as she found Leandro Herrera? How long since she'd felt that spark?

She turned her head, just slightly, so she faced him. Saw understanding dawn in those gorgeous dark eyes. And then his mouth touched hers. The lightest, sweetest contact. It made her mouth tingle, made her want more.

She moved a little closer, and felt his breathing change.

And then he was kissing her again. Tiny, nibbling kisses, persuading her to open her mouth and let him deepen the kiss.

She completely forgot the music. Forgot to

dance. Forgot to move. The only things she was aware of were the feel of his mouth against hers and the desire scorching through her. She couldn't remember the last time she'd felt like this—maybe since the early days with Michael. Although she'd dated a couple of times since her divorce, she'd never wanted it to go further than a goodnight kiss, and a chaste one at that.

With Leandro, she wanted more. A lot more.

And she wanted it now.

From the feel of his hard body against hers, she knew it was completely mutual. That he wanted her just as much.

At last he broke the kiss. '*Em sap greu.* Sorry. That wasn't supposed to happen.'

She felt her face heat. And the way she'd reacted, kissing him back… He must think she was a complete tart. They were almost strangers, and she'd practically thrown herself at him. 'I'm sorry.' She swallowed hard. 'I'll go.'

'I don't want you to go. I didn't mean that.' He stroked her cheek. 'Just that when I invited you to dinner, I didn't expect you to sleep with me in return.'

Her face heated even more.

'Which isn't a polite way of saying that I'm not attracted to you. I want you, Becky. Very much. But I don't want you to feel that I'm pressuring you. So I'll call you a taxi.' He moistened his lower lip with the tip of his tongue. 'Because if you stay here for much longer I'm not going to be able to be an honourable man. My self-control will splinter and I'll end up carrying you to my bed.'

The idea made her whole body quiver; she could feel her nipples hardening at the thought. Being carried to Leandro's bed. And he'd be as good a lover as he was a dancer. Looking out for her, making sure her pleasure was as great as his.

But there was a problem. A huge one. Because she didn't want her heart broken again. She'd been there when her marriage had broken up—and then, just when she'd thought she'd reached the lowest point, she'd discovered she could hurt even more.

And she was never, ever going to take that kind of risk again.

Work, at least, was safe. Something she was good at. Something where she could make the world a better place.

She dragged in a breath. 'There's something I should tell you. I'm not looking for a relationship.'

'I'm not looking for a relationship either. I'm about to start a new job.' He spread his hands. 'I don't have time for anything except my work.'

So if they did this, it would be for one night only.

One perfect night with a stranger.

Tempting. So tempting. But even if this was going to be just for one night, she didn't want him thinking badly of her. She didn't want him thinking that she made a habit of going off with complete strangers. 'I don't do one-night stands, as a rule.'

He inclined his head. 'Then I'll respect your wishes and call you a taxi.'

It would be the sensible thing to do.

But after the days she'd spent in London and the miserable day at work, Becky needed warmth. Needed to *feel*.

She shook her head. 'I don't want you to call a taxi.'

Her words came out in a whisper, and Leandro's pulse quickened. 'You want to stay here with me?'

She nodded.

'Just for tonight.' He needed this to be clear. He'd already seen what relationships did to people—he'd grown up knowing that his mother's heart was cracked in two. And he wasn't going to let that happen to him. So he'd concentrated on work: keeping his relationships for fun and his heart intact. Despite the physical pull he felt towards Becky Marston, that wasn't going to change. His focus was on his career, and it was going to stay that way.

'Just for tonight,' she confirmed.

Heat flared at the base of his spine. 'You're sure about this?'

She lifted her chin. 'I'm sure. Very sure.'

He bent his head and kissed her. Hot and hard. And when he lifted his head he could see desire reflected in her eyes. *Ets molto atractiva.*

'Sorry?'

Idiot. He needed to remember she didn't speak Catalan. 'I said,' he translated softly, 'you're beautiful.' He stole another kiss. 'You should know, I don't make a habit of this.'

'Neither do I.'

'I didn't think you did.'

She swallowed hard. 'And there's something else you should know. I'm a bit out of practice.'

She didn't say so aloud, but he could read it in her eyes—she was worried that she'd disappoint him.

He smiled and rubbed the pad of his thumb along her lower lip. 'That isn't a problem. I have a feeling that this is going to be good—for both of us.'

CHAPTER THREE

LEANDRO took Becky's hand and led her to the stairs. Then he stopped, looked at her, said something in rapid Catalan and scooped her up with one hand under her knees and the other round her waist. She slid her arms round his neck for balance, and he carried her up the stairs as if she were a slender five-foot waif instead of curvy and five feet seven.

It should've felt macho and offputting.

Instead, it sent a kick of desire through her. That this gorgeous man wanted her so much he couldn't wait to carry her to his bed.

He pushed the door open with his foot, then set her back down on her feet next to the bed before going over to the window and closing the curtains.

Tonight she was acting out of character, but she wasn't going to be completely reckless. 'Do you have protection?'

He nodded. 'I have protection. *Not* that I was planning this to happen tonight,' he added. 'My suggestion of dinner meant just that: dinner.'

'Think of this an unexpected bonus,' she said softly.

He walked back over to her and brushed his mouth against hers. 'For both of us, *estimada.*' He switched on the bedside light and came to stand behind her, wrapping his arms round her waist and pulling her back against him. He dipped his head and kissed the nape of her neck. 'You smell lovely,' he said softly. 'Like chocolate.'

And so she should: the expensive bubble bath Tanya had given her for her birthday smelt of chocolate. She felt the warmth of his mouth against her nape again.

'Mmm. You taste of chocolate, too,' he murmured. 'And I'm hungry.'

She knew exactly what he meant. Although they'd just eaten, she too was hungry.

Not for food.

For him.

And the way he was kissing her neck was the most arousing thing she'd ever experienced in her life.

He eased himself away from her for just long enough to undo the zip of her black shift dress. Slowly, so slowly, and his mouth traced a path down her spine as he uncovered her skin. When he reached the fastening of her bra, he un-snapped it, then slid the straps of her dress over her shoulders, drawing the straps of her bra down at the same time. As the fabric fell to her waist, he drew a line of kisses from the curve of her shoulder to the curve of her neck—tiny, open-mouthed kisses that made her want more.

She spun round to face him, letting her dress and her bra fall to the floor. Lord, his mouth was beautiful. If she could sculpt, she'd definitely want him as a model. She reached up on tiptoe and kissed him; as he responded, letting her explore his mouth in turn, she undid the buttons of his shirt and slid her palms across his pectoral muscles.

Perfect musculature.

She kissed her way down his throat, nipping gently and feeling a surge of satisfaction as he couldn't suppress an 'oh' of pleasure.

Half-dressed, he was gorgeous. He had smooth olive skin, with a scattering of dark hair across his chest—enough to be sexy but not so much that it was offputting.

She'd just bet that, at the beach, he turned heads. Of women who wanted to be with him—and men who wanted to *be* him.

She pushed the material off his shoulders, letting his shirt pool next to her dress on the floor. 'You're beautiful,' she said softly. 'I take it you work out at the gym?'

'No.'

She drew her fingertips down his arms. Again, perfect musculature without a hint of flab. 'You feel like someone who takes care of his body, not a couch potato. So if you don't go to the gym, you must do some kind of sport.'

He nodded. 'I run most mornings. And I fence.'

She felt her eye widen. 'With a sword?'

'A foil,' he corrected her.

She could imagine him as a Spanish pirate on a ship, swashbuckling his way through danger. Or even better, in eighteenth-century France with tight black trousers and a ruffled shirt. 'I can see you as one of the Three Musketeers.' She slid her fingers though his hair. 'With long hair, you'd look amazing.'

His eyes glittered with amusement. '*Gràcies*—but I don't think that would go down too well with my boss.'

'What do you do?' she asked, suddenly curious.

He shook his head. 'I don't want to talk about work tonight—right now it's just you and me and I want to make love with you, Becky. I want to kiss you. Now.'

She tipped her head back slightly in invitation, and he wasn't slow to take her up on it. His mouth was warm and strong against hers, and his tongue slid into her mouth, mirroring the action his body would make later.

I'm kissing a stranger, she thought. One of the most gorgeous men I've ever met, one who's cultured and can dance and cook—but he's still a total stranger. This is crazy. I really shouldn't be doing—

Then she stopped thinking as his hands slid up to cup her breasts. When the pads of his thumbs rubbed against her hardened nipples, she gave a sharp intake of breath.

He drew back slightly so he could look her straight in the eye. 'You like that?'

'Yes.'

He gave her a lazy grin. 'Good.' He repeated the action, and she shivered. But it still wasn't enough. She wanted more.

As if he could read her thoughts in her eyes, he traced a trail of light, teasing kisses down the sensitive cord at the side of her neck; the caresses turned to hot, open-mouthed kisses against her throat when she arched back and closed her eyes. He moved lower, kissing a line down her sternum, and a pulse beat hard between her legs; the beat grew even stronger when he shifted slightly and drew her nipple into his mouth. As he sucked, she gasped in pleasure, sliding her fingers back into his hair and urging him on.

Becky was past all coherent thought when Leandro dropped to his knees in front of her, removed her tights and stroked her inner thighs until her stance widened, then slid one finger under the edge of her knickers and drew it along the length of her sex. She could feel the warmth of his breath against her inner thigh. If he didn't touch her properly now, she'd go crazy. Implode.

He pushed one finger inside her, and she couldn't help crying out.

'OK?' he asked softly.

'N-no.'

To her shock, he removed his hand. 'I'm sorry. I'll go into the bathroom and leave you to get dressed. Just give me a few minutes to cool down.'

What? No! That wasn't what she wanted at all. 'That isn't what I meant.' Her voice was low and breathy and just a little bit fractured.

He frowned. 'No means no.'

'I meant, no, I'm not OK. I...' She took a deep breath. 'I want more.'

Enlightenment dawned and he gave her a slow, sexy smile. 'More, hmm? Tell me.'

She felt the colour stain her cheeks. 'I want you to...to touch me.'

'Here?' He stroked the backs of her knees, keeping his gaze trained on hers.

She shivered. 'North a bit.'

His smile widened and he stroked her inner thighs. 'Here?'

'North a bit,' she said again.

He laughed. 'You do realise you're giving me two-dimensional directions?'

'Then how...?' She couldn't think straight.

'Show me.' His voice was low and sent heat

flickering down her spine. 'Show me where you want me to touch you.'

Oh, lord. Everything she'd ever heard about Latin lovers was true.

And Leandro Herrera made her blood fizz.

She placed her hand over his and drew it up until he was cupping her sex, still through her knickers. 'Here.'

'Just here?'

A tiny murmur of frustration escaped from her. 'Don't tease me.'

He smiled. 'I'm not going to tease you, *estimada*. I'm going to make love with you. And I want to take it slowly.' Again, he circumvented her knickers, but this time, instead of pushing a finger inside her, he used his fingertip to brush lightly against her clitoris, skating back and forth until her knees went weak and she grabbed his shoulders with both hands, afraid that she was going to fall over.

'I'm not going to let you fall,' he said, guessing her fears. 'Well, not in *that* way.'

She closed her eyes as he continued caressing her and the pleasure built higher, higher.

And then he stopped.

She opened her eyes wide and stared at him in disbelief. Why had he stopped now, when she was so near the peak? 'Leandro?'

'I want your eyes open,' he said. 'I want you to see me. And I want to see your eyes.' With his free hand, he removed her knickers and looked up at her. '*Madre de Deu,* Becky,' he said softly. '*Ets bella. Te desitjo.* I want you.' He punctuated every word with a tiny movement of his hand that had her quivering. Just the right pressure and the right speed.

And then, unbelievably, her climax hit. Wave upon wave of pleasure.

'Oh-h-h. Leandro. *Yes.*'

Little aftershocks of pleasure were still rippling through her when he pulled his duvet aside, lifted her, and laid her gently against the pillows.

'Thank you. That was…' She couldn't find the right word. 'Amazing.' More than amazing.

He slid her a sultry look. 'I haven't finished yet.'

And then she realised he was still wearing his trousers. While she was completely naked. Abandoned.

She felt her eyes widen. 'You're—'

He stopped her protest with a kiss. 'It's OK. I

wanted the first time to be for you. And, as I said, I haven't finished yet.'

Oh, lord. If he could reduce her to a quivering heap with just one finger, what would it be like when his body finally slid inside hers?

He undressed swiftly. Gracefully—well, as a fencer, of course he'd be graceful. And Becky sucked in a breath as she saw him naked for the first time. 'You're perfect.'

'*Gràcies.*'

He joined her on the bed and traced the curve of her jaw with a fingertip. 'And you, too. Curvy, not a stick insect.' As she instinctively sucked in her stomach, he smiled, leaned over and traced a circle round her navel with the tip of his tongue. 'I said "curvy", not "fat". A real woman. *Mateia bella.* Very beautiful,' he translated, rummaging in his bedside drawer for a condom.

He took it out of its foil wrapper, rolled it on, then slid his hand between Becky's thighs and teased her with his clever fingers until she was quivering again. 'Now?' he asked.

'Oh-h-h. Now. Yes. Please.' She couldn't remember the last time she'd wanted a man so much. It had been years.

Leandro knelt between her thighs, gently fitted himself to her entrance and then eased in, in one long, slow thrust.

She'd forgotten how good making love could be. How long had it been?

But, no, she didn't want the bad memories to seep in and spoil this. Live for the moment, she reminded herself. And this moment was good. Really, really good.

She stroked his back, his buttocks—lord, his gluteal muscles were as perfect as his pectorals—and then, when he ran one hand lightly up her thigh and cupped her buttocks, she wrapped her legs round his waist. Took him deeper.

Every thrust took her nearer and nearer the edge.

'Look at me, *estimada*,' he reminded her softly.

She did. And at the precise moment her climax hit again, she could see it reflected in his own eyes, in the way his pupils dilated until his eyes were almost completely black.

He wrapped his arms round her, holding her close and muttering words in Catalan which she didn't understand, though his tone told her he was as moved by what had just happened as she was.

Eventually, Leandro withdrew. 'Excuse me for a moment,' he said politely.

She knew he needed to deal with the condom, but as he left the room she started to wonder what the protocol was here. She'd never had a one-night stand before. Should she stay or should she leave now?

Just as she was about to get out of bed and find her clothes, so at least she'd be dressed when he came back and wouldn't feel quite so embarrassed about discussing it, he returned to the room—completely naked and uninhibited by his nudity—smiled at her and joined her in the bed.

'I'm glad you didn't decide to go.' He put his arm round her, drawing her close so her head was resting on his shoulder. 'I know we said neither of us want a relationship, and that hasn't changed. But stay with me for a while.'

This was what she'd missed even more than sex. Being cuddled.

Being held as if she were someone precious.

Something that had definitely been missing from the last months of her marriage.

And the silence wasn't uncomfortable; she didn't feel the need to break it. Right here, right now, in Leandro's arms, she felt warm and safe and wanted.

Her eyelids started to drift down; although she knew she really ought to leave, maybe a few minutes' nap wouldn't hurt...

She stopped resisting and fell asleep.

CHAPTER FOUR

BECKY woke feeling warm and comfortable. Then she remembered it was Sunday morning and she was on a late shift. Which meant that she could have a lie-in: she could just drowse and go back to sleep.

And then two things burst into shocking clarity.

Firstly, this wasn't her bed.

And, secondly, she was wrapped spoon-style around a hard male body, her face against his back and her arm slung comfortably round his waist.

Leandro Herrera.

Her gorgeous Catalan lover—for one night.

Oh, lord. She really shouldn't have stayed. They'd both said this wasn't going to be a relationship. She should've taken a taxi home last night.

From the regularity of his breathing, she knew that he was still sound asleep. Well, that was hardly surprising. They'd spent much of the night exploring each other, finding out just where each other liked to be stroked or kissed.

Forget the lie-in. She needed to leave. *Now.*

Slowly, cautiously, she slid her arm from around his waist and wriggled backwards. Leandro stirred for a moment, then rolled over onto his front.

Lord, he was gorgeous, she thought. A perfect back, broad shoulders and good muscle tone, and that beautiful smooth olive-toned skin. She was, oh, so tempted to kiss her way down his spine. Wake him up nicely.

But she knew what would happen next—and she'd end up being late for work. Which wouldn't be a good idea.

In some respects, she really regretted what she was about to do. Physically, she and Leandro were compatible. Very compatible. He was the most beautiful man she'd ever seen. But, more than that, she'd enjoyed his company last night. Leandro was good to talk to, he was a great cook, and she'd felt comfortable with him.

Though the sensible side of her knew this was the right thing to do. Make a clean break. They weren't going to see each other again. And even though she was tempted to break her personal rule and maybe see where their relationship took them, she didn't want to end up in the same mess as last time—involved with a man who wanted completely different things out of life and expected her to make all the compromises. Because although Leandro seemed more domesticated than Michael had ever been, there were limits: Leandro had made it clear the previous night that his new job was going to take up all his time. Just like Michael, Leandro would be focused on his career. His job would come first, and hers...

Well, Michael had made it clear that her job wasn't as important as his. And Becky had done with compromising.

She wasn't prepared to give up all the years of studying and hard work she'd put into her career. She wanted to go right to the top. To become nurse consultant, and then maybe nursing director; she enjoyed helping develop her junior staff almost as much as she enjoyed treating patients.

So she dressed quietly and swiftly before tiptoeing out of Leandro's bedroom and down the stairs. Although she could do with a shower, she didn't want the noise of the water to wake him. Besides, it wouldn't take her long to get home and she'd have plenty of time for a shower there.

Though she wasn't going to vanish completely without saying goodbye—she'd been brought up to be polite.

If you could be polite with someone who'd given you mind-blowing sex the previous night.

She rummaged in her handbag for her personal organiser and removed a blank page. She wrote him a note and propped it against the kettle where he was bound to see it:

Thank you. Sorry, had to leave. B.

And she *was* sorry. Sorry that she couldn't give Leandro a chance. But she had good reasons not to want to get involved, and no doubt his reasons for not wanting a relationship were equally sound.

'Be happy,' she said softly, glancing up the stairs, and let herself out of the house, closing the door quietly behind her.

Becky had assumed that Tanya, being on a

day off, would still be asleep. So she crept into her own house as quietly as she'd crept out of Leandro's. But when she'd clicked the door shut and turned round, Tanya was standing in the hallway. Fully dressed. And, unlike Becky, Tanya wasn't wearing the same clothes she'd worn the previous night.

'So where did you get to, then?' her house-mate asked with a knowing grin.

Becky smiled back. 'Morning. I wasn't expecting you to surface until this afternoon.'

'It wasn't that late a night.' Tanya laughed. 'Though the same clearly can't be said for you, you dirty stop-out.'

Becky groaned. 'Enough with the teasing.'

'I know you sent me that text saying you were going to dinner with that guy from the party—but are you telling me you actually spent the night with him?' She frowned. 'I was a bit worried about you when I got your text.'

Becky flushed. 'OK, so it was a bit of a rash thing to do. But I told you exactly where I was going and who I was with. And I kept my phone switched on. And I'm never going to take a risk like that again.'

'He must've been really something,' Tanya mused, 'for you to break the habit of a lifetime.'

Yes. Leandro *had* been really something.

'Actually, it probably did you good,' Tanya continued thoughtfully. 'You've dated such utter losers since Michael—and don't give me that look, Rebecca Marston. You know you have.' She put her hands on her hips. 'It's because you're scared of commitment—you always date dreadful men who couldn't possibly have a future with you so they're absolutely safe to go out with.'

'Hey, I thought you worked in paediatrics, not on the psych team,' Becky said lightly. Though she knew her friend had a point: she *was* avoiding commitment. One unhappy marriage was enough for her. She wasn't interested in a second chance at failure—or giving her family another stick to beat her with. 'And I have to have a shower and change or I'll be late for my shift. Catch you later, OK?'

Tanya clapped a melodramatic hand to her chest. 'So you mean I don't get any of the gory details? None whatsoever?'

'Nope.'

'Spoilsport.' Tanya rolled her eyes, but let her go.

When Becky she arrived at the hospital for her shift, she found the usual Sunday afternoon mix waiting for her—pulled muscles and sprains from people playing sports, plus backache from gardeners who'd made the most of the sunshine but had overdone things after a winter with no real digging, and small children who'd stuffed beads up their noses. Some of them she had to refer to the doctor, but most of the minor injuries she could deal with herself.

And the best thing about her job, she thought, was that people left with a smile. They came in to the department worried sick or in pain, and left knowing what was wrong with them and with the injury treated.

But at the end of the shift she still couldn't get the gorgeous Catalonian man out of her head.

Maybe she should contact him.

After all, she hadn't given him any of her details, so he had no way of contacting her—but she knew exactly where he lived...

No. Best to leave it as a fabulous memory, no complications.

To her relief, Tanya didn't bring up the subject of the beautiful stranger that evening. Becky was on a late shift again the following morning, and when she walked into the changing room Irene, one of the staff nurses, was on her break.

'Hi. Nice day off yesterday?' Becky asked.

'Brilliant. Lee and I went to my parents for the day. I love family get-togethers. I mean, we ended up having the kids all sitting round a pasting table for Sunday lunch and the rest of us crammed in around the dining table, but that didn't matter because we had such a laugh. And Mum, bless her, always makes my favourite pudding—even though it's three years since I lived at home.'

How different other people's lives were, Becky thought. And how nice it must be to look forward to visiting your parents, knowing there were going to be warm hugs and conversation, instead of silences, accusations and looks of disappointment. Grandparents who spoiled you and made a fuss of you, instead of criticising everything from your dress sense to your career.

Maybe she should've divorced her family at the same time as she'd divorced Michael.

She shook herself. 'So dare I ask what the new consultant's like? Up to David's standard?'

'Yes.' Irene fanned herself. 'And I can see why Human Resources kept the information to themselves.'

Becky frowned. 'You've lost me.'

'Because there would've been queues of nurses—not to mention all the female doctors—who suddenly needed emergency treatment, and really needed to see our new consultant personally,' Irene said with a grin. 'He's *gorgeous*. If I wasn't happily married, I'd be tempted.'

Becky rolled her eyes. 'Don't tell me. Tall, dark and handsome?'

'That doesn't even begin to cover it. We're talking definite sex-god status.' Irene eyed her speculatively. 'Actually, you could…'

'No, I couldn't,' Becky corrected with a smile. 'Work and relationships don't mix. And, anyway, he might not be my type.'

'Box of chocolates says you fall for him,' Irene said immediately. 'And I'm talking about a big box. My favourites—Belgian seashells.'

'No way.' Becky laughed. 'I couldn't be so

mean. You're on a definite loser there—it'd be like taking sweeties from a baby.'

Irene tapped her nose. 'You just wait until you meet him. You'll change your mind.'

'He's probably married, with kids. He must be at least in his thirties.'

'No, no and yes. Karen—' the department's senior receptionist, who knew practically everything about everyone '—asked him. But... No, I'm not going to spoil the surprise.' Irene grinned. 'You just wait.'

'Yeah, yeah.' Becky changed into her uniform and took the handover from Sarah, the nurse practitioner who'd been working in the minor injuries unit during the morning.

There was no sign of their alleged sex-god consultant.

Not that it bothered her—she was more interested in doing her job.

Her next patient was a builder. According to the initial notes taken by the triage nurse, he'd slipped from scaffolding while working on a building site, and one of his fellow builders had brought him in.

'So it's your right ankle, Mr Barker,' she said as he limped in. He could clearly bear weight on it, so that was a hopeful sign that it would turn out to be a sprain rather than a fracture. 'Take a seat. Can you tell me what happened?'

'Slipped off the scaffolding—I was only a couple of feet up.' He rolled his eyes. 'Talk about stupid.'

'Easily done,' she said sympathetically. 'How did you land?'

'My right foot went under me—it felt as if I twisted my ankle.'

'And how does it feel now?'

'Throbs, and hurts like hell when I try to stand on it.'

'Do you mind if I examine you?'

'Sure.' He grimaced. 'Sorry about the boots. They smell a bit. I've got sweaty feet.'

She smiled at him. 'Trust me, we've had far worse in here.' Gently, she examined his ankle. 'I'm pretty sure it's a sprain, but because of the way you landed I'm going to send you for an X-ray, just to make sure. Before I do, I just need to ask you a few questions, if you don't mind.' She quickly took his medical history, checked that he wasn't on any medication, gave him some ibuprofen to help with the swelling and pain, and wrote out a form. 'If your friend can help you down the corridor to the X-ray department, take this form to the reception area and they'll sort you out. Then come back here and I'll see you when the results are back.' She smiled at him. 'Sorry about the wait.'

'That's all right, petal.'

She wrote up the notes and called in her next patient. Judging from the wet teatowel wrapped round the woman's hand, she'd guess at a burn.

'Can you tell me what happened, Mrs Tennant?'

'I can't believe I were that stupid,' Mrs Tennant said, looking exasperated with herself. 'I'd put the kettle on and I reached into the cupboard to get the teabags. My daughter's home from school with a stinking cold and she called out to me—and I just stood there with my arm stretched over the kettle, not thinking, when I called back to find out what she wanted. Course, I moved me arm the minute I felt the heat, but it were too late.'

'When did it happen?'

'Half an hour back. I got a taxi. My neighbour did first aid at work and she put a clean wet teatowel over it, and she said I ought to come here because it's my hand.' She bit her lip.

'She's looking after my Jessie. I hate putting other folk out, but she said there were nowt for it but to come here.'

'I'll be as quick as I can, then,' Becky promised.

'Don't I have to see the doctor?'

Becky shook her head. 'I'm a nurse practitioner. That means I've done extra training so I can prescribe things and treat certain injuries. If I think it's more complicated, I can call a doctor through,' she explained. 'May I take a look?'

Mrs Tennant nodded. 'It hurts like mad.'

'That's a good sign—it's when it *doesn't* hurt that it's more likely to be serious,' Becky said. 'Not that it helps you right now—but I can give you something for the pain.' Gently, she examined the burn—the skin was red and blistered, moist to the touch, and the redness had a mottled pattern. Added to the pain that Mrs Tennant had referred to, and the fact that it was a scald rather than a chemical or thermal burn, she knew exactly what she was looking at. 'You've got a partial-thickness burn to your wrist. The blisters might get a bit bigger but try very hard not to burst them, because the fluid inside is keeping the area sterile,' she explained.

'It might be a good idea to take off your wedding ring.'

'I never take it off,' Mrs Tennant said, looking horrified.

'With a burn,' Becky said quietly, 'sometimes the area swells up. If your fingers swell up, it's going to be pretty uncomfortable. It'll only be for a few days—and it's better to take your wedding ring off now and keep it safe than to have to have it cut off in a couple of days' time.'

Mrs Tennant nodded, and took off her ring.

'What I'm going to do is cover the area with silver sulphadiazine cream and put a dressing on. I'll give you some dressings to take home, and you need to change them every day,' Becky said. 'It's a good idea to wash your hand in warm salty water, but don't use antiseptic. I'm going to make you a follow-up appointment for three days' time so we can have a look at how it's healing—but if you notice it's getting redder or more painful, or it smells a bit odd, or you've got a temperature, it means there's an infection in the burned area and you need to see your GP or come back before your appointment.'

Mrs Tennant nodded. 'It hurts a fair bit, though.'

'It'll be sore for a while, so you can take paracetamol for the pain—but no more than eight in twenty-four hours,' Becky warned. 'The good news is that it should heal in a couple of weeks and won't leave a scar, though you might notice your skin's a bit darker in that area.'

Once she'd arranged the follow-up appointment for Mrs Tennant, Becky checked the computer to see if Mr Barker's X-rays were back yet. The hospital's picture archiving and communication system meant that scans and X-rays could be seen on any computer screen in the hospital, and that saved a huge amount of time.

She was pleased to see that the pictures were available—and even more pleased to see that the X-rays were clean.

'Mr Barker?' She called him back into the treatment area and showed him the screen. 'You'll be relieved to know you don't have a fracture. It's a bad sprain, so what you need to do now is to remember RICE—it stands for rest, ice, compression and elevation.'

'You've lost me, petal,' he said with a smile.

'You need to rest your ankle—put ice on it for ten minutes or so every hour, use an elastic bandage to support it except when you go to bed, and keep your ankle raised so it's above the level of your hip. And it's a good idea to try to move it around in all directions to help stop the muscles seizing up. This is a good exercise—if you can copy what I do?' She showed him some gentle circular exercises and checked that he was able to make the same movements. 'It's going to hurt for a while so you can take pain-killers—ibuprofen or paracetamol are both fine. The good news is that you should make a complete recovery in a fortnight or so.'

'So I can't play footie?'

''Fraid not.' She smiled ruefully. 'Sorry.'

She continued seeing patients until she went for her break at half-past four. There was still no sign of the new consultant. Becky assumed that he'd gone for the day—if he'd been on an early, his shift would've finished a while back. Never mind. She'd try and introduce herself to him tomorrow.

But what she really wanted right now was a cup of coffee.

She pushed the door of the rest room open—and stopped dead when she saw who was sitting there.

CHAPTER FIVE

IT COULDN'T be.

Becky blinked hard and looked again.

Yes, she definitely recognised the man sitting there in the rest room.

But what on earth was Leandro Herrera doing at the hospital? Had he tracked her down, wanting an explanation of why she'd left?

Her next thought was relief that it was just the two of them in the rest room—because this was a conversation she definitely didn't want over-heard. She knew what it was like to be the focus of the hospital grapevine, and she really didn't want to repeat the experience.

'*Hola*, Becky,' he said quietly.

'What are you doing here?' she asked, closing the door behind her.

'The same as you, I assume.' He shrugged. 'I work here.'

The penny dropped. '*You're* the new emergency department consultant?' Now she understood why he'd been invited to Joe's party. Because of the unsocial hours they worked, medics tended to be friends with other medics, so at a party the guests tended to be either colleagues or neighbours. Given that Leandro lived in a much more upmarket district than Joe did, she really should've guessed which category he fell into.

'Yes.' He paused. 'So why didn't you wake me up yesterday? Why did you leave without a word?'

Because she'd panicked.

Because she hadn't known how to deal with the situation.

Because...

'Look, it was awkward,' she said, embarrassment flooding through her. 'What happened on Saturday was out of character for me. I don't normally do that sort of thing.' She'd been driven by a mixture of wanting to celebrate life after losing a patient and wanting to run wild after feeling so trammelled in London.

He said nothing, simply folded his arms and stared at her.

She sighed. 'All right. I apologise for not waking you and saying goodbye personally. But I did leave you a note. It was propped up on your kettle.' A nasty thought struck her. 'You *did* see it, didn't you?'

He inclined his head. But he still looked unimpressed.

'It was polite,' she protested. She'd said thank you. And apologised that she'd had to leave. What more had he expected? 'Look, we'd agreed it was for just one night, and I was due on shift here, and…' Her eyes narrowed as she realised he hadn't seemed surprised to see her. She looked at him. 'Did you know I worked here?'

'Yes. But only since this morning. Irene's been singing your praises—how we have this fabulous nurse practitioner who's really good at dealing with patients in the minor injuries section, and she always makes time to develop staff and teach them new things.'

Becky felt herself colour. 'I'm just doing my job.'

'Nurse practitioner.' He looked thoughtful. 'Whose role is to facilitate the minor injuries service, lead a team of emergency nurses, and maintain effective relationships with the emergency team.'

She didn't like where this was heading—or the gleam in his eye. 'That's *working* relationships,' she pointed out.

'Exactly.'

She had a nasty feeling she'd just landed straight in a trap. And that feeling increased when he added, 'And now you're working with me. As I'm new here, I could do with a briefing on the department.'

'I'm sure Irene's already filled you in.'

'But Irene isn't on the senior nursing team,' he pointed out.

Whereas she, as nurse practitioner, most definitely was.

She needed to get out of this situation. Fast. She glanced at her watch. 'Sorry, I'd love to help you, but I'm afraid I'm due back in minors.'

'What are you doing after your shift?'

The question caught her on the hop. If she invented something, she had a feeling he'd know she wasn't telling the truth. So what did she say? Admit that she was going home to curl up on the sofa in front of her favourite TV drama, which Tanya would've recorded for her?

When she said nothing, he said softly, 'I assume you're going to need to eat.'

'I'm on a late shift. I don't finish until gone eight.'

'Not a problem. As you know, I'm used to eating late.'

He wasn't going to let her wriggle out of this, was he?

And her thoughts must have been written all over her face because he smiled. 'Becky. We'll be working together and we need to talk.'

To set out some ground rules? she wondered.

'So—your office or mine?'

'How to make the hospital grapevine run riot,' she muttered. She already knew their new consultant was single. And that he was very, very eligible. And the rumour factory would be more than happy to speculate about the relationship between the new consultant and the nurse practitioner.

'I could have made it go mad earlier,' he pointed out. 'I could have gone up to the paediatric ward, found Joe and asked him if he knew where I could find Becky Marston. People would've overheard the question, added two and two together and made ten. Because people probably saw us leave that party together.'

'This feels like blackmail.'

'Hardly,' he said, one corner of his mouth quirking slightly.

Oh, lord. His mouth. She could remember the touch of it against her skin, the feel of it against her own mouth. And the memories sent heat flooding through her.

'You're part of the senior nursing team. It's natural that I should discuss departmental business with you—and as you have a reputation for good team-building, it follows that, of course, you'll be happy to talk to me outside shift hours.'

'About work.'

He shrugged. 'What else?'

Personal stuff. And the look in his eyes told her he was thinking about that, too. 'I'm not in the market for a relationship,' she reminded him.

'Neither am I. And this isn't the best place to discuss it. Not if you want to avoid the hospital grapevine. *Fins després.*' At her slight frown, he added, 'See you later.'

Her body still remembered how it felt to be

touched by him, the warmth of his mouth and the sureness of his hands. And his accent… Although his English was perfect, he spoke with a slight Catalan accent and it was so damn sexy. When he actually spoke Catalan to her, it made her quiver. Remembering what he'd said to her on Saturday night.

Te desitjo.

I want you.

Oh-h-h.

'Becky?' he asked, looking concerned.

Which probably meant she had a goofy expression on her face. Brilliant. Not. 'Catch you later,' she said, and went back to the minor injuries unit without her coffee.

She just about kept her mind on her job for the rest of her stint in minors, and then it was time to catch up with paperwork in her office. But even before Leandro knocked on her open door, her whole body tingled with awareness of him.

Oh, help.

This really hadn't been meant to happen.

She didn't need a complication like this in her life.

* * *

Leandro stood in the doorway, watching Becky work. She was concentrating on the computer screen and working through a pile of paperwork next to her—an extremely neat pile, he noticed, and there was nothing out of place on her desk. Becky Marston was a woman who juggled her responsibilities well and would make it a point of honour not to let anything slip—her patients would always come first, but she'd also look out for her staff.

He was about to knock when she looked up and met his gaze.

And it felt as if a current was flowing through him. Heat. Sparkle.

He'd done his share of dating and he'd always managed to keep his love life light and flirty and fun, but he'd never felt a pull this strong towards anyone before. In some respects, he knew that meant he ought to give Becky Marston a wide berth. She was dangerous. He was here on secondment for six months, and a relationship was absolutely not on his agenda. Even if he ended up agreeing to extend the secondment, he still wasn't looking for anyone permanent in his life. There wasn't room.

And yet he couldn't resist the temptation of spending some time with her.

This might be dinner, but primarily it was *work*, he reminded himself. Though at the same time his body tightened, remembering what her bare skin had felt like against his. How she'd tasted. Her scent.

He pulled himself together. '*Hola*, Becky. Ready?'

She looked up and wrinkled her nose. 'Can you give me five more minutes, so I can just finish this bit of paperwork, please?'

'Sure.' He was the same: he didn't like leaving things unfinished. Which was one of the reasons why he was in England in the first place. Something deeply personal—and a solid reminder of why he didn't do relationships. Because they were a hell of a lot less secure than a career.

'Do you mind if I wait here?' He gestured to the chair next to her desk.

'That's fine.'

Ha. She was being polite and formal with him. Professional. But he'd seen a different side of her. One he thought that very few people in the hospital—if any—had seen. Not Becky the nurse: Becky the woman, all warm and soft and giving.

And he really had to stop thinking about it before he did something rash. Like spinning her chair round to face him and kissing her stupid.

He sat quietly, glancing around her office. Everything was neat. All the nursing manuals and box files were lined up and in a sensible order. Her desk was neat, with an in-tray, a filing tray—which was empty, so clearly she kept on top of things—plus the computer and a little silver mesh pot that held her pens.

On the cork board on the wall next to the desk everything was neatly pinned in its place. The duty rota for the next two weeks, a typed list of emergency contact numbers for the nursing staff and senior doctors, and an equally neat list of phone numbers for various departments. A couple of postcards from exotic places, which he guessed had been sent by colleagues.

But there was nothing personal. Nothing that told him anything about Becky herself. No photographs framed on her desk or pinned to her board—not even pictures from departmental nights out, the kind of thing he'd seen on the pinboards of other offices.

Rebecca Marston obviously kept a very clear line between her personal life and her work life.

Which was what he ought to be doing, instead of speculating what it would feel like to kiss her again. She was his colleague, and he didn't date colleagues: the sheer speed and volume of work in the emergency department put enough pressure on a team without the added complication of relationships.

'Right. I'm done. Sorry to keep you waiting.'

'De res,' he replied with a smile.

She logged off, switched off the computer and locked her desk, then stood up and gestured to the door. 'Shall we go?'

'Sure. So where do you recommend?'

'Depends what sort of food you like.'

He smiled. 'I'm easy to please.'

He noted that her colour heightened slightly at the words. Clearly she was thinking about pleasure. About what they'd done on Saturday night. About how he'd pleased her—and how she'd pleased him.

He should stop this right now.

So why the hell couldn't he?

'There's a little *trattoria* round the corner,' she said. 'It's quiet and the food's good.'

'Sounds fine to me.'

She kept the conversation firmly on work as they walked to the little Italian restaurant, right up until their coffee arrived.

And then she looked at him. 'We're going to be working together.'

'Yes.'

'So it's a professional relationship.'

'That would be the sensible thing,' he agreed.

'But?' Clearly she'd heard his doubts in his voice.

'You don't do one-night stands, and neither do I. The fact that we did, on Saturday night…'

'Means nothing.'

It didn't feel like nothing. And that was what really concerned him. He wasn't used to feeling like this. And it bothered him that he was even considering breaking his personal rules and getting involved with a colleague.

'Look, I'd had a bad day,' Becky continued. 'I'd lost a patient—and you'd just moved here and were at a loose end.'

'You sound as if you're trying to convince yourself as much as me.'

'I'm not looking for a relationship,' she insisted.

'Did he hurt you that much?'

'Who?'

He knew she knew perfectly well who he was talking about. 'The man who put you off relationships.'

She sighed. 'My marriage turned out to be a disaster, and most of it was my fault.'

Why was she taking the blame? 'It takes two to make a relationship.' And usually two to break it. Unless she'd had an affair—and, although he didn't know her well, his instincts told him that Becky Marston wasn't the type to treat her marriage vows lightly.

'I really don't want to discuss it.'

'*D'acord.* All right. I won't push you. But…' He grimaced. 'This is crazy. I don't do this sort of thing. But there's something about you. Something that makes me want to…' He shook his head, unable to find the right words. But there was one thing he was sure of. 'And I think it's the same for you.' The way she'd looked at him when she'd opened the door to the staffroom. Shock. Hunger. Desire. And then closing herself off, putting professional distance between them.

'I don't know what you mean,' she said.

Though she didn't meet his gaze. And he couldn't resist the challenge. He reached across the table, took her hand and drew it to his lips. He kissed each knuckle in turn, and then replaced her hand on the table. 'Look me in the eye and tell me that didn't affect you.'

'It didn't affect me,' she said immediately.

'Right. So how do you explain the fact that your pupils are enormous?'

'The lighting level isn't that high here. It's a physiological reaction to let more light into my eye.'

He spread his hands. 'It's also body language. The sign of physical attraction to someone. The pupil dilates up to four times its original size— and women's pupils dilate faster than men's.'

She frowned. 'You're an emergency specialist. How come you know about body language?'

'Misspent youth.' He raised an eyebrow. 'You also brushed your hair away from your face when you talked to me.'

'Because I need a haircut and it was getting in my eyes.'

He smiled. 'In terms of body language, women flick their hair to show a man they care about how they look to him. It also exposes their armpit enough to release pheromones.' He nodded at her cup, which she was turning round and round in her hands. 'And you're fiddling with a cylindrical object.'

She flushed beautifully, getting his point straight away. 'This is ridiculous.'

'Absolutely,' he agreed. 'We're both single, neither of us have any ties. Neither of us wants a permanent relationship. And I don't usually date anyone in my department because it makes life too complicated. But...'

'But?'

'I find you attractive, Becky. Very attractive. And your body language tells me you feel the same way about me.' He rested his elbows on the table, propped his chin on his joined hands and looked at her. 'I don't think this thing between us is going to go away. So it's going to be much easier to work with it than to fight it.'

'So what are you suggesting? A fling, to get it out of our systems?'

'Yes.'

She shook her head. 'I don't—'

'Do this sort of thing?' he finished. 'Neither do I. I don't proposition women. The same way that you don't go off with a stranger at a party and spend most of the night making love with him.'

'That's below the belt.'

'But also true.'

'Hmm. You know why I'm single. What about you?' she asked.

'I'm thirty-five years old and I've been a consultant for three years. What does that tell you?'

'That you're dedicated to your job.'

'Exactly.' He'd been promoted quickly because he was good at his job and he'd been very, very focused on his career. 'A lot of people can't handle that. The fact that you're going to put your job before your relationship. That you want to build your career and make something of yourself.'

For a moment, something flickered in her face. But it was gone before he could be sure.

'Why did you decide to work in England rather than Barcelona?'

He sidestepped the question, not ready to tell her about his search for his father. His search for the truth about the past. 'I'm here on secondment. For six months, with the option of extending it to a year.'

She looked thoughtful. 'So if they're keeping David's place open for him...that means you're a locum.'

'A long-term locum, if you like. But, yes, it's not permanent.' He spread his hands. 'As I said, you're not looking for permanence and neither am I.'

'So you're suggesting an affair. No strings.'

'An exclusive affair.' He looked at her, unsmiling. 'Which means neither of us dates anyone else.'

'Technically, an affair isn't dating.'

That made him smile. 'Actually, I had something more in mind than just sex. I meant spending time with you. Having dinner. Listening to music. Wandering round museums. Maybe going for a walk in the country somewhere—I assume there are parks or something nearby?'

She nodded. 'There are parks in Manchester, but if you want to go outside the city there's Alderley Edge—it's mainly woodlands but there

are a couple of points at the top where you get
to see right across Cheshire to the Peak District.
It's where they used to mine copper in prehis-
toric and Roman times.' Her eyes lit up. 'Or if
you like wandering around old houses, there's
Tatton Park. Or Chester—there are all the half-
timbered buildings in The Rows. And the zoo.'

'Then we'll go to all of them.'

The light in her eyes faded, turned to worry.
'This is beginning to sound like a relationship.'

'No. We're colleagues. And maybe we'll
become friends.' He paused. 'But we'll also
have a little something extra. Just between us.'

He noted that her pupils dilated just that
little bit more.

'Friendship with something extra.' She
paused. 'So if I say yes, what then?'

'I drop you home, and we see each other some
time when we're free.' He raised an eyebrow. 'I
suppose I could kiss you stupid on your front
doorstep and give your neighbours something to
talk about…'

'No! And especially not in front of Tanya.'

'Your housemate,' he recalled.

'She works in Paediatrics. And she knows as

many people as Irene does.' Her expression turned serious. 'If we do this—and I mean *if*—then this is just between us.'

'You really think we're going to be able to keep it a secret in a hospital?'

'Well, probably not,' she admitted.

He lifted her hand again and pressed a kiss into the palm. 'What shift are you on tomorrow?'

'Early.'

'That's a killer after a late.'

'The shift pattern's normally two earlies, two lates, two nights and two off,' she said, 'but I swapped duties with a couple of people so I could get the days off I needed last week.'

'When you went to London to see your family.'

Her face shuttered straight away, and he remembered that she'd said something about having to go back for a family birthday. Clearly she had as many issues with her family as he did with most of his.

'I apologise if I spoke out of turn,' he said softly.

'It's not you. I'm just a bit…' She paused. 'Well, let's just say I'm not close to my family.'

'Believe me, I know exactly how you feel,' he said dryly. 'I have the grandparents from hell.'

'Tell me about it,' she said.

'You, too?' At her grimace, he said, 'Let's not let the bad stuff get in the way of the good.'

She nodded. 'Sounds like a good plan.'

'So may I drop you home? My car's in the hospital car park.'

'Thanks. It'll be nice not to wait for the bus.'

'You normally take the bus?'

'I don't need to run a car. I can get the bus or train anywhere I need to go. Well, most places,' she said. 'Right, this bill's mine.'

'No. Dinner was my idea.'

'I pay my way.'

Had that been an issue in her marriage? he wondered. She was so fiercely independent. 'How about I pay for dinner tonight, and you pay next time?' he suggested.

The silence stretched, then finally she nodded. 'All right. Thank you.'

He smiled. *'D'acord.'*

He paid the bill and walked with her through to the hospital car park.

'What?' he asked, when he saw the way she looked at his car.

'I was expecting—well, most of the consultants I know drive much flashier cars.'

'If you have a garage to put it in, fine. I don't. And the weather in England isn't like the weather at home—there's no point having a convertible if you can only have the roof down for one day a year.'

'So you're a practical man, Mr Herrera.' She sounded approving.

He smiled, and opened the passenger door for her. Before she could protest, he said softly, 'In my country, we still believe in good manners. I know you're perfectly capable of opening your own door, but you're my passenger. So. No arguments, *d'acord?*'

'*D'acord.*'

He loved the fact she'd bothered to speak his own language. And although their journey back to her house was relatively silent, it was a relaxed silence. He parked the car, then switched off the ignition.

'Thank you for this evening,' he said quietly. 'I'm not expecting you to invite me in—apart from the fact that Tanya might be there, you have an early shift tomorrow and need your sleep.'

She nodded. 'Thank you for understanding.'

He took her hand and raised it to his mouth.

Brushed his lips across her wrist. *'Fins demà,'* he said softly. 'See you tomorrow. Sleep well.'

'Goodnight, Leandro.' For a second she pressed her palm against his face. And then she climbed out of the car.

He waited until she'd closed her front door behind her before driving off. Tomorrow, he thought, had just become full of promise.

CHAPTER SIX

BECKY was working in Triage the next morning when Leandro came over to her. 'Becky, I need you with me in Resus—the ambulance crew just called through. They'll be here in five minutes. They're bringing in an elderly woman with severe abdominal pain and vomiting.'

'Do you know her history?' she asked.

'Just that she's here visiting her daughter. Nobody else in the family's affected, so it's unlikely to be food poisoning. Her daughter's coming in with her, and maybe she can help fill in the gaps for us.'

Ed, the paramedic, told them a little more when he brought the patient through to Resus on the trolley. 'Mrs Sturman has a temperature of about forty degrees, her blood pressure's on the low side, and she's delirious. I've given her an antiemetic and paracetamol.'

'Thanks, Ed.' Leandro smiled at him. 'And you must be Mrs Sturman's daughter, yes?'

The middle-aged woman, who looked distraught, nodded. 'Erin Crosby. What's wrong with her?'

'That's what we're going to find out. There are a lot of conditions that could cause your mother's pain and sickness.' He held the old lady's hand. 'Mrs Sturman? My name's Leandro Herrera and I'm the consultant here. Would you mind if I examine you?'

'I just feel so awful,' Mrs Sturman moaned.

'I know, and we're going to do our best to make you feel better,' he said gently. He turned to the younger woman. 'Can you tell us anything about your mum's medical history, Mrs Crosby? Does she take any tablets?'

'She's a diabetic, but she doesn't need insulin and I'm careful what I give her—not too much fruit or carbs, and definitely not cake or biscuits.' Erin smiled wryly. 'Mum's got a bit of a sweet tooth, so it's an uphill battle.'

Leandro nodded sympathetically. 'And it's hard when everyone else can eat what they like, I know.' He gently examined the elderly woman. 'I think she's having a thryrotoxic crisis.'

'But there's nothing wrong with her thyroid,' Erin protested.

'A thryrotoxic crisis can be caused by other medical conditions—if her blood sugar's too low, or she's had a heart attack or been in an accident or even had some kind of infection,' Leandro explained. 'Becky, I need an urgent blood screen.'

'Thyroid function tests, full blood count, blood glucose and blood culture,' she said immediately, having already assembled the syringe and collected the bottles. 'And I'll get Kayleigh to organise a chest X-ray.'

'Mrs Sturman, Becky needs to take a blood sample from you so we can run some tests,' he said quietly. 'May we have your consent?'

The elderly woman nodded.

'We also need to check your arterial blood gases—it will hurt a little bit more than a normal blood test, and I'm afraid I can't give you a local anaesthetic for it. But can you be brave for me?'

A tear rolled down her cheek, but she nodded again.

'That's good.'

Becky held the old lady's hand while Leandro took the sample for the blood gases, soothing her gently all the while.

'Thank you. You did really well,' Leandro said. 'And I'd like to examine you now. Would you mind if my assistant Mina listens through the stethoscope? We also need to take a reading of the electrical activity of your heart—what we call an ECG. It's not going to hurt—it's just putting some electrodes on your chest.'

'Your assistant…she's a student?' Mrs Sturman croaked.

'She's passed her exams and qualified, but this is her first year in the hospital—what we call a foundation doctor. And…' he leaned forward '…she's very bright and very kind.'

That was true of Leandro himself, Becky thought as she labelled the samples. He'd reassured their patient and her daughter, put the clinical picture together swiftly, and she guessed that he was already working out the treatment plan. And Mina was pink with pleasure at the compliment.

Mrs Sturman agreed to let Mina assist and to have the ECG.

'Thank you,' he said again. He listened to her heart, then moved the stethoscope to just over Mrs Sturman's thyroid gland.

Becky knew exactly what he was checking for, and her thoughts were confirmed when he said to Mina, 'Listen to this and tell me what you hear.'

The junior doctor did as he asked, then said, 'It sounds like a murmur.'

'Exactly—thyroid bruit. It's caused by increased blood flow.'

Meanwhile, Becky set up the ECG.

'See that wiggly line?' he said to Mrs Sturman, showing her the trace. 'That means your heart's beating in a normal rhythm but it's beating too fast. So what I want to do now is to give you some medication to make your heart slow back down to a more normal rhythm. The best thing for me to prescribe for you is a drug called Propanol, but I can only do that if you don't suffer from asthma. I know it's hard for you to talk right now, so I'll ask your daughter to put me in the picture, if I may?' At the elderly woman's nod, he turned to Erin. 'Mrs Crosby, do you know if your mother has ever suffered from asthma?'

'No—nobody in the family has it,' she replied.

'Good.' He held the elderly woman's hand. 'You're doing really well here, Mrs Sturman. I'm going to give you Propanol to help your heart, plus a small injection of something called heparin, which will thin your blood a little and make sure you don't develop a blood clot.'

She nodded, and another tear trickled down her face.

'You're doing really well,' Becky said gently. 'And I can see you're still hot, so I'm going to sponge your skin to help you feel a bit more comfortable.' The paracetamol clearly hadn't kicked in yet and she needed to do more to bring Mrs Sturman's temperature down. Tepid sponging was one of the best ways. She went to fetch the water from the basin in the corner while Leandro talked to Mrs Sturman about her treatment plan.

'I think you have a thyrotoxic crisis—it's a hormonal problem which means your body's producing too much thyroxine and it's affecting your heart rate. The blood tests will confirm it but I want to start treating you now. I'm going to give you a medicine called carbimazole, which will stop the thyroxine synthesising in your body, and Becky and Mina will work with me to get your temperature down and your blood pressure back up.' He held Mrs Sturman's hand and smiled reassuringly at her. 'We'll have you feeling better soon.' He turned to face Mrs Crosby. 'Your mother is going to be fine, but I'd like to admit her so we can keep an eye on her for tonight. We'll see how things go, and if my colleagues on the ward are happy, maybe she can come home again tomorrow.'

The younger woman looked relieved. 'Thank you.'

'I'll have a word with the bed manager,' Becky said, 'and I'll fill in all the forms, then I'll take you both up to the ward and introduce you to the team who'll be looking after your mum. Kayleigh,' she said to the student nurse, 'can you continue with the tepid sponging, please? Keep an eye on Mrs Sturman's temperature and keep Mr Herrera informed of any changes.'

'Will do,' Kayleigh responded.

They were busy with another emergency that took them up until lunchtime, and Leandro had a meeting with the hospital's clinical director. It wasn't until Becky's break in the afternoon, after Mrs Sturman had been admitted to the ward and settled in, that he caught up with her.

'I'm not going to patronise you by saying well done, but it's a joy to work with someone who's so intuitive. I don't have to explain everything to you or ask for things, because you know exactly what you're doing.' He smiled. 'And, trust me, I've worked with enough people who need their hands held through every single procedure.'

'Anyone listening to you would think you were an ogre,' Becky said lightly. 'And you were good with Mina, who still needs a bit of hand-holding.'

'Because she's a relatively new doctor and she still has a lot to learn. Which isn't the same as being experienced but leaving other people to make all the judgements.' He shrugged. 'I'm still young enough to remember my first rotation in the emergency department and I'm not going to make it any harder for Mina than it is already.'

'That was David's approach,' she said, sounding approving. 'We've been lucky with our senior doctors—there's none of the arrogance I've heard friends in other departments complain about.'

'What's the point in being arrogant? It just makes people not want to work with you. And in a department like this we need to work together, for our patients' sakes.'

'True.'

'The department here has an excellent reputation. I made the right choice, coming here.'

'So what made you come from Barcelona to Manchester?' she asked.

To find the man who might be his father—the man who'd broken his mother's heart. To get answers to the questions that had been haunting him for half a lifetime. To understand *why*.

Though he wasn't quite ready to share that. 'Personal reasons.'

'In other words, back off?'

She was quick. And she also looked hurt that he'd put up a barrier between them. *'Em sap greu.* I'm sorry, I didn't mean to snap at you.' He raked a hand through his hair. 'I'm still getting my head round something, that's all.'

'Would it help to talk?'

'On the basis that you're a medic, so whatever I say is confidential?'

She nodded.

He smiled and took her hand, squeezed it gently. '*Gràcies,* Becky. But I'm not ready to talk. Not yet.'

She squeezed his hand back. 'I won't push you. But that's what friends are for.'

'A friend who's holding my hand,' he remarked.

'Ah, no. This is exactly what I'd do to a patient who was upset about something. It's a gesture of sympathy.'

'While they're in pain, yes. But I'm not in pain and you're still holding my hand.'

'Fair point.' She disentangled her fingers from hers. 'Someone might come in.'

'And if they come into the rest room and see me kissing you, that's not such a good idea,' he said ruefully. He really shouldn't have said the k-word. Because right now he really, really wanted to kiss her. Feel her mouth soften under his.

He wasn't used to feeling an attraction this strong. On the one hand, it made him want to bolt for the safety of his office. And on the other, it made him want to break all his personal rules.

He'd already broken one, by dating someone in the same department. And they were meant to be seeing each other casually. But he still couldn't help asking the question. 'Have dinner with me tonight?'

'Sorry, I can't. It's my aqua-aerobic class. I go with Tanya,' she explained, 'and it's not fair to her if I drop out at the last minute.'

'What shift are you on tomorrow?'

'Nights—and I'm on a night on Thursday, too.'

'Which means that Friday and Saturday you have off?' he asked.

'Yes.'

'Then maybe we can spend Friday afternoon together. If I pick you up at two, that'll give you a chance to have some sleep first. If it's raining we'll go to a museum or the cinema, and if it's fine maybe we can go somewhere for a walk.'

'I'd like that.'

'And, Becky?'

'Mmm-hmm?' She looked up at him, her dark blue eyes clear.

Knowing he was taking a risk but unable to resist it, he dipped his head and brushed his mouth against hers. 'Just to remind you,' he said softly.

She shivered. 'I have a very good memory.'

Yes, and her pupils had dilated hugely. Which meant that this was affecting her exactly the same way it affected him. 'Good. Keep remembering that,' he said. 'I'll see you later.'

That kiss left Becky smiling all the way home. And despite the fact that the aqua-aerobics teacher gave them a harder workout than she'd had the previous week and her legs definitely felt like jelly afterwards, she couldn't stop the smile. Couldn't remember the last time she'd felt this happy. They'd set the ground rules and she trusted Leandro to stick to them. Everything was going to be just fine.

At least, until the hospital grapevine found out about it.

But she'd deal with that when she had to. For now, she was just going to enjoy this.

She half expected her housemate to have heard something, but to her relief Tanya didn't even mention the new consultant until they were sitting in the fitness complex's café after their class with a latte and a muffin.

'Sophie tells me she had to come down to

your lot today and she saw the new Spanish consultant—she reckons he's sex on legs.'

'Actually, he's from Catalonia.'

Tanya frowned. 'Eh?'

'He's from Barcelona.'

Tanya rolled her eyes. 'Ye-es. As I said. Spanish.'

'Catalonia is part of Spain,' Becky explained. 'It's kind of like calling a Scotsman British— it's technically correct but you'll offend his national pride.'

'Got you. So, is Sophie right? Is he drop-dead gorgeous?'

Yes. 'If you like the tall Latin type,' Becky hedged.

'What's he like to work with?'

'He's a nice guy. He doesn't patronise the patients or look down on the nursing staff or throw his weight around. We've been pretty lucky—he's taking exactly the same approach as David did.'

'So what's his name again?' Tanya asked.

Uh-oh. This was where it was going to get a little bit difficult. 'Leandro.'

Tanya stared at her, her jaw dropping as she

made the connection. 'You're *kidding*. Not Mr Saturday Night?'

Becky felt her face heat. 'Um, yes.'

Tanya gave her a sympathetic smile. 'Ouch. That must be difficult for you—your new boss being the man you had a one-night stand with.'

'First of all, he's not my boss. You know as well as I do that the nursing staff don't report to the doctors,' Becky reminded her. 'And as for the rest of it—that's fine. We're both completely professional.'

Tanya raised a speculative eyebrow. 'So does this mean he's *not* going to be just a one-night stand, then?'

'Oh, give me a break, Tan. I worked really hard in that aquafit class and I'm starving. I need carbs—and this raspberry and white chocolate muffin's sitting there saying, "Eat me, eat me now."'

'Stop trying to change the subject, Becky.' Tanya's grin widened. 'You haven't denied it, so you *are* seeing him, aren't you?'

Becky squirmed. 'Look, it's not what you think…'

'No, because he's not one of your usual

losers.' Tanya reached across the table and gave her a swift hug. 'Good. About time, too. Welcome back to the world.'

Becky rolled her eyes. 'Don't be so daft. I haven't been away from the world.'

'Yes, you have. And, with any luck, you'll realise now what you've been missing!'

Becky didn't see Leandro before her shift the next night, but she knew he was around. Because he'd left her an envelope in her in-tray. An envelope which looked as if it contained bulky reports or notes but which actually contained a tiny box, in which nestled four very posh chocolates. The kind of gift that was small enough to be acceptable because it was so obviously without strings; but it also sent her another message. That he was thinking of her. That he remembered what she liked.

He'd left a sticky note on top of the box. *Have a nice shift. L.*

After a gesture like that, all hell could break loose and she'd still have a good shift—because he'd made her night brighter.

During her break, Becky looked up a Catalan

dictionary on the internet and cobbled together an email. *Gràcies per il xocolatas. Són bonic.* Thank you for the chocolates. They're lovely.

Even though she knew her grammar was probably wrong, he didn't pick her up on it— he merely sent her another envelope with another little box of chocolates the next night. This time the first half of his note was in Catalan: *De res. Fes-me un petó el divendres.* He'd added a PS in English. *My mobile phone number, in case you need to get in touch. L.* He'd written the number underneath.

He had strong, spiky handwriting. Confident and bold, like Leandro himself. But, unusually for a doctor, Becky thought with a smile, his handwriting was also legible.

It took her a while to look up the various words in the Catalan dictionary on the internet, but she got the general sense of it and laughed. *You're welcome. Give me a kiss on Friday.*

It took her a while longer to find the phrase she wanted, but eventually she found it and scribbled it on a sticky note. On her second break, she went into the corridor and sent him a text message on her mobile phone. *Ets molt divertit. Becky.*

You're very funny.

I ets molt simpàtica was his response when she checked her phone the next morning after her shift—she didn't need to use an online dictionary to get the gist of that message. He'd added, this time in English, *See you at two.*

She smiled. Right now, she didn't feel like sleeping. She felt like dancing on air. And she could hardly wait until two.

CHAPTER SEVEN

BECKY set her alarm for half-past one. The weather forecast was, for once, for sunshine, so if they were going for a walk she wouldn't need to dress up. And half an hour was enough time to have a shower, wash her hair, pull on a pair of jeans and a long-sleeved T-shirt, and have a cup of coffee.

At precisely two, the doorbell rang. When she opened the door to Leandro, her pulse started to beat faster. Dressed in snug faded jeans and a black round-necked sweater, topped with a pair of dark glasses and the sexiest smile she'd ever seen, he looked absolutely edible.

She tried her best to sound cool and calm. '*Hola*, Leandro.'

'*Hola*, Becky.' He leaned forward and stole a kiss. The light touch of his mouth against hers sent a tingle all the way through her.

'Ready?'

'Ready,' she confirmed. 'I just need to get my handbag.'

It didn't take long to collect her handbag and lock the door behind her. Again, Leandro insisted on opening her passenger door.

'You really don't have to.'

'Yes, I do. And I'm doing your seat belt up, so leave it.'

Oh, no, he wasn't. She had her seat belt fastened before he'd even opened the driver's door.

'Spoilsport,' he said.

She frowned. 'What do you mean?'

'I wasn't being old-fashioned or a control freak. It was the brilliant excuse I had lined up.'

'Excuse? For what?' she asked, mystified.

'To do this.' He leaned over to touch the point where the clip of the seat belt would have hung, had she left it. Close enough for her to feel the warmth of his body. Close enough for her to smell the scent of lemons on his skin—obviously from the shower gel he'd used earlier. 'And then this.' He cupped her face. 'And then this...' He proceeded to kiss her very slowly and very thoroughly. To the point where she felt as if all her bones had melted.

Then he pulled away just far enough so he could see her face. 'Big pupils, husky voice, very red and slightly swollen lips... I'd say the lady liked that.'

'You're such a comedian.'

He laughed. 'You're the one who told me I was very funny. And in my own language, too.'

'I got it right?'

'The second one, yes. The first one...well, I knew what you *meant* to say.' He smiled at her. 'But I'm delighted that you made the effort. Far be it from me to be picky about grammar. Unless, of course,' he said ruminatively, 'you want me to teach you. And you pay me a kiss per correction. So you owe me two for that one—should've been *ils* and *bonics*, both with an S.' He leaned forward again and stole a kiss. 'That one's on account. The other I'll collect later.' He put his own seat belt on. 'So. Where would you like to go?'

'You said a walk if it was a nice day. Alderley Edge would be fantastic.'

'Alderley Edge it is.' He tapped instructions

into his satnav, then headed south of Manchester until they reached the village.

'So where do you suggest?' he asked when they left the car.

'The Wizard's Walk,' she said. 'You get to see the wells and the two places where you can look from the top of the Edge over Cheshire—on a day like today, the view will be fabulous.'

'Sounds good to me.' He smiled and took her hand. 'You know the way. Just tell me where to turn.'

It felt odd to be walking hand in hand with someone. She couldn't remember the last time she'd done that with Michael. While their marriage had been disintegrating, physical contact between them had reduced until it had been practically nothing. Although Leandro clearly felt the tension running through her and gave her a searching gaze, to her relief he didn't ask any questions.

She loved walking here, especially when the sun was shining and the birds were singing. And by the time they'd reached Stormy Point, she was thoroughly relaxed and didn't protest when he sat down and pulled her onto his lap. 'This is beautiful, *estimada*,' he said softly. 'What an amazing view. Thank you for suggesting this.'

'*De res*,' she said with a smile.

'I think it's time for another lesson. Repeat after me, *Fes-me un petó, si us plau*.'

'I know what that means. I looked it up.'

'Uh-uh,' he warned. 'You don't argue with your teacher. Say it.'

This was a complete and utter set-up, and she knew it. And she really enjoyed his playful side. Just being with Leandro made her smile. '*Fes-me un petó, si us plau*,' she said.

'Of course I'll give you a kiss, Becky,' he said with a grin, 'seeing as you asked me so nicely.'

What started out as a light, teasing brush of his lips rapidly turned into something much hotter and deeper. And when he broke the kiss, Becky was quivering. 'Oh-h-h. Leandro, this is a public place. I really think…'

He nuzzled the curve of her neck. 'You're absolutely right. We should stop. While we still can. But you do something to me, Becky. *Mai ningú m'ha fet sentir el que ara sento per tú*,' he added in Catalan.

'Are you going to translate that?'

His answer was a hug. 'I don't think you're ready for that particular translation just yet. Come on. Let's finish our walk.' He gently shifted her off his lap, climbed to his feet and pulled her up next to him. 'And you can tell me why this is called the Wizard's Walk.'

'There are three wells,' she said as they set off towards them. 'The holy well, the wishing well and the wizard's well. The wizard's well—oh, you'll see it when we get there. But I loved the story behind it when I first heard it.'

'Tell me,' he invited.

'A farmer was riding his white horse across the Edge to sell it at Macclesfield Fair when suddenly the horse stopped and refused to move. An old man with a staff suddenly appeared and wanted to buy the horse, but the farmer refused, thinking he'd get more money for it at the fair. But nobody bought the horse, so on the way home, when the stranger appeared again, he agreed to sell the horse. The wizard took him to a huge rock, which turned into iron gates.' She paused. 'See that rock over there? That's meant to be the one.'

'In legend, of course,' Leandro said, smiling

at her. 'And let me guess—he took the farmer to some treasure?'

She nodded. 'And he also saw sleeping knights in full armour with a white mare beside each one. The wizard told the farmer that in England's darkest hour they would wake and do battle on the plain below Alderley Edge—and then he told the farmer to take as much gold as he could carry and leave. Just as the farmer stepped through the gates, the iron clanged shut and the rock crashed back together again. And although he tried to come back and find the place again, he never found it.' She smiled at him. 'The locals think that the wizard was Merlin and the knights were from King Arthur's Round Table—though that's probably because the Cornish tin miners came to work up here and brought their legends with them.'

'I used to love the King Arthur stories when I was a boy,' Leandro said softly. 'My mother used to read them to me. Sometimes I used to pretend my dad was a knight on a white charger and he'd come back for me and my mum.' He shrugged. 'Not that he ever did.'

Although his tone was light, Becky could tell

that his feelings ran deep. Leandro's dad had obviously left and the old hurt still had raw edges. And she was beginning to understand why Leandro concentrated on work rather than his personal life: if you grew up seeing unhappy relationships, you either tried to prove that it'd be different for you and rushed into marriage without thinking it through properly, or you steered well clear. She'd done the first, and now she was doing the second.

Well, trying to.

Though this thing with Leandro wasn't a relationship. They'd both agreed that. It would be over when he went back to Barcelona.

Having a time limit made it safe.

She squeezed his hand. 'Having two parents isn't necessarily all it's cracked up to be,' she said softly.

'Your relationship with your parents is difficult?'

She nodded. 'Having grown up with years of having to be careful what I said in case it sparked off yet another row between my parents… I sometimes wish I'd grown up with just one parent. One who didn't argue with other people all the time.' She grimaced. 'Sorry, this isn't about me. You're close to your mother, aren't you?'

'*Sí*. She always made time for me. And she always believed in me—she worked two jobs to help put me through medical school. So I owe her more than I can ever repay.'

She'd just bet that Leandro's mother loved him all the way back. That he was the apple of her eye. And for a moment she really, really envied him. What would it be like to be loved unconditionally—loved for who you were, faults and all?

But this wasn't the place to be melancholy.

'I bet she's so proud of you.'

'And I am proud of her.' His fingers tightened round hers. 'Look, I don't have a chip on my shoulder about not having a father.'

'Though it's made you wary of relationships.'

He shrugged. 'Let's walk.'

In other words, he didn't want her to push it. Fair enough. She didn't like talking about the things that had gone wrong in her life either. But she still wondered whether Leandro had avoided marriage because he worried that he'd be like his dad and walk out if things got tough.

They admired the view from Castle Rock, and then headed down to the wizard's well.

'So how old is this carving?' Leandro asked, peering at the carving of a man's face.

'I don't know. A couple of hundred years maybe. But the words were probably carved a bit later.'

'"Drink of this and take thy fill For the water falls by the wizard's will,"' Leandro read. 'It looks as if the water runs down the rocks and into the trough. Is it safe to drink?'

'I wouldn't risk it,' she said. 'I've heard it contains traces of lead.'

'Not sensible, then.' He raised an eyebrow. 'Is there a café anywhere around here?'

'There are several in the village.'

'Good. All this walking has made me thirsty.'

'For a nice cup of English tea?' she teased.

He pulled a face. 'No. Coffee. Or water. But tea...now, that's an acquired taste. How you English drink so much tea, I will never know.'

When they reached the café, Leandro looked at Becky. 'Do you think it would be possible to have an English cream tea with coffee rather than tea?'

She laughed. 'I don't see why not.'

'Will you join me?'

'That'd be lovely. Thank you.'

He placed their order and they'd just settled in to their seats when there was a loud crash. The waitress, who'd been carrying a tray of drinks and cakes, had tripped over someone's bag. When she'd put out a hand to stop herself, she'd dropped the tray. But, more worryingly, when she'd fallen she'd landed on one of the glasses, which had shattered, and blood was seeping over her skin.

Leandro immediately sprang to his feet and was there in two strides, helping her up. 'I'm a doctor. Let me look at that for you,' he said. He sucked his teeth. 'It looks as if there's still glass in there. That needs to be seen to in hospital.'

'Hospital? But I can't— My aunt...' the waitress began.

'We can't take the glass out here,' Becky said gently, 'because the fragments cut on the way out as well as on the way in, and we don't want to make your arm worse.'

'Ashleigh, what have you...? Oh, my God!' the woman bustling in from the back room said.

'She tripped and landed on some of the glassware. We need to get her to a hospital to get this treated properly,' Leandro said. 'By the time we've called an ambulance, we could have driven her to the emergency department our-selves—our car is just outside. I'm a doctor—Leandro Herrera—and Becky Marston here's an emergency nurse practitioner,' he said, 'so Ashleigh will be in good hands.'

'I'd better get a bandage,' the woman began.

'Better not,' he said gently. 'We don't want to put pressure on the wound and drive any glass in deeper.'

'Ashleigh, honey, this might sting a bit, but I'm going to press along the side of your wound rather than on top of it. That'll make the bleeding stop,' Becky said, performing the pro-cedure as she talked Ashleigh through it. 'And you need to raise your arm.'

As well as the danger of further damage from the glass, she was concerned that Ashleigh might go into shock.

'We'll ring you from the hospital,' Leandro promised. 'We'll get your number from Ashleigh.'

Becky supported Ashleigh to Leandro's car, still putting pressure on the edges of the wound, while

Leandro rang the ward to say they were bringing in someone who needed to be seen urgently.

'What about your car? There'll be blood everywhere!' Ashleigh protested.

'It's really not a problem,' Leandro reassured her, helping her into the back seat of the car. Becky got in next to Ashleigh so she could continue to look after her and monitor how she was doing—the last thing the poor girl needed was to go into hypovolaemic shock—and then Leandro drove them straight to the hospital, parked in his usual space, and he and Becky took Ashleigh to the emergency department.

Becky noticed that the girl's face was getting paler and paler. 'Are you all right?' she asked.

'Ye-es,' Ashleigh said, not sounding it at all. 'It's just…our neighbour went into hospital last year. She didn't come out again. She got MRSA.'

'It's pretty rare,' Becky said softly. 'And we've stepped up hygiene precautions to help stop it happening. There are gel dispensers all over the place so people can make sure their hands are clean.'

'Would it help if we were the ones who treated you?' Leandro asked. 'You trust us, don't you?'

The girl nodded.

'OK. We'll stay with you and we'll treat you,' Leandro promised.

They took her through to the cubicles.

'Hey, I thought you two were both meant to be off today?' Irene said.

Leandro smiled. 'Emergency doctors never really go off duty. Even when they're off, they're…well. This is Ashleigh. She's got a nasty cut with glass in it. And she doesn't like hospitals, so she agreed to come if we treated her. I did ring in.'

'Yes, there was a note. I'll go and sort out the paperwork,' Irene said.

In the cubicle, Ashleigh sat on the bed and Leandro switched the lamp on so he could see what he was doing. 'I'm just going to check that you can feel things where you should be able to feel them,' he said gently, 'and then I'm going to give you a tiny, tiny injection of local anaesthetic to stop it hurting.'

'Injection?' Ashleigh's eyes widened.

Becky squeezed her hand. 'I promise, you won't even feel the scratch. Leandro is *really* good with needles.'

Leandro examined the area, and was clearly satisfied that there wasn't any sensory loss because he then drew up a syringe of lignocaine. 'Look at Becky and smile,' he directed. 'And I want you to count backwards in threes from twenty-eight.'

'Twenty-eight?' Ashleigh swallowed. 'Um, twenty-five…' She paused, clearly concentrating. 'Twenty-two.'

'All done,' he cut in gently.

'But…I didn't feel it.'

'That's why I asked you to count for me. So you'd have something else to think about and you wouldn't be all tense, waiting for the needle to go in and worrying that I was going to hurt you.' He smiled at her. 'Your arm's not going to be so sore now. I'm going to take out the glass I can see, then I'm going to send you for an X-ray to check all the glass is out. If it is, then I can stitch up that cut—and you won't feel any of the stitches because I've numbed the area.' He irrigated the wound with sterile saline solution to wash out all the grit, then took a pair of tweezers and removed the glass. 'I think we're there now.'

'I'll take you through to X-Ray,' Becky said.

'Take the glass with you,' Leandro said. 'They can X-ray that at the same time to see if the glass shows up on the scan. If it does, then we can be sure that if any glass is still in Ashleigh's arm then it will show up.'

And if it didn't…that would mean more physical exploration of the wound. But Becky kept that to herself. Ashleigh was scared enough without having to deal with that prospect.

When they were back from the scan, having confirmed that all the glass was indeed out, Leandro sutured the wound. Becky was impressed at the speed and neatness of the stitches.

'I'm going to put a dressing on, more to protect your arm than anything else,' she told Ashleigh, and took over when he'd finished suturing.

'I'll call your aunt to let her know that you're OK,' Leandro said. 'And we'll take you home—unless you'd rather go back to the café?'

'I'd rather go to the café, please,' Ashleigh said quietly.

'Sure. Now, you'll need to come back and have the stitches out in a week or so, and we can see how your wound's healing at the same time. If it goes red or inflamed or it hurts a lot, you need to go to your GP because it means you have an infection,' Leandro explained, 'but hopefully it shouldn't be too much bother.'

When they'd dropped Ashleigh back at the café and reassured her aunt, they went back to the car.

'Sorry,' Leandro said. 'Our afternoon out wasn't meant to be quite like that.'

She smiled. 'You're a doctor and I'm a nurse. We're hardly going to leave someone to suffer when we can do something to help, are we?'

'No. But we may have a teensy problem to deal with.' He grimaced. 'Irene wanted to know why we were both at the café. I told her we were having coffee and a discussion about work. Except obviously Ashleigh's address was here in Alderley Edge.'

'And Irene always puts two and two together and makes six.' Becky smiled ruefully. 'And she's going to demand a huge box of Belgian chocolates from me.'

'How so?'

'Before I knew you were our new consultant, she bet me a box of chocolates that I'd fall for you. I said no because it'd be like taking sweets from a baby—she'd lose.'

He laughed. 'Now, that's cut my ego down to size.' Then his smile faded. 'So are you telling me you just lost the bet?'

That she'd fallen for him? She wasn't prepared to admit that just yet. 'We have this friendship thing. With, um, something extra.'

'Ah. That. Which she will interpret as you losing the bet.' He leaned over to kiss her. 'Then I will have to make it up to you, *estimada*. Do you have plans for this evening?'

'Not really. Tanya's on a late and she's going straight out from work with her team.' She paused. 'I could cook dinner for us, if you like.'

'I'd love that.'

'It'll be pot luck—whatever's in the fridge,' she warned.

He put his lips very close to her ear. 'I can be *very* inventive,' he drawled.

A shiver of pure lust surged through her at his words. 'Leandro!'

'I meant cooking,' he deadpanned.

'Sure you did.' She smiled at him. 'Let's go, then.'

CHAPTER EIGHT

BECKY'S house wasn't quite what Leandro had expected. The walls were bright and the prints on the wall were very modern—though from what she'd told him he already knew she liked traditional art. So the pictures were her house-mate's taste perhaps? He also noticed that all the photographs on the mantelpiece were of Tanya with people who looked enough like her to be her family; there were none of Becky with hers. Even the photographs of departmental nights out on the pinboard in the kitchen seemed to be mainly of Tanya and her crowd. If Becky had been there, too, clearly she preferred to be behind the camera rather than in front of it.

But why did she keep herself closed off like that?

The woman he was getting to know was warm and giving. She was well liked and respected at work—he hadn't heard a single criticism of her, not even a tiny one. So why the barriers?

Whatever the reason for her marriage breaking up, it had clearly hurt her deeply—so deeply that she wasn't prepared to have another relationship. She'd only agreed to see him because he was on secondment and there was a foreseeable end to his stay in England—which would also signal the end of their relationship.

Right now, that suited him. He didn't want a commitment getting in the way of his career. And yet the way he felt around Becky was... Well. He didn't want to think about it too deeply and give it a name. But it unsettled him. Because it wasn't something he was used to.

Together, they cooked a meal, though Leandro noticed that Becky didn't switch on the radio in the kitchen. He usually had music on all the time. 'So you're not that keen on music?' he asked as they sat down to eat at the kitchen table.

She flushed. 'I like stuff you can sing to—pop. I don't have highbrow tastes.'

She thought he was a music snob because he'd played her Mozart? He smiled. 'There's nothing wrong with pop. I like stuff you can sing to as well.'

Though she still didn't switch on the radio, even when she stacked the plates on the worktop while he filled the bowl with sudsy water ready to do the washing-up. And he began to wonder if she was compartmentalising him, too. Just to test it, he scooped some suds onto his fingertips and dabbed them on the end of her nose.

She looked at him in utter shock, her eyes and mouth widening.

He grinned, and loaded up for a second shot.

Except her reactions were quicker than he'd expected—she scooped the suds off his fingertips and splattered them on his sweater.

'Oh, so you're upping the stakes, are you?'

A full-scale water fight ensued. None of the washing-up got done, but by the time they'd finished his sweater was wet and her long-sleeved T-shirt was clinging to her curves.

'OK. You win the Ms Wet T-shirt competition,' he said, smiling.

She laughed. 'The whole concept of a wet T-shirt competition is so un-PC, how can you possibly call it "Ms"?'

'If a wet T-shirt offends you, we could always…' Before she had a chance to guess what he had in mind, he'd tugged the hem of her long-sleeved T-shirt over her head.

'Mmm, a much better view.' Lord, she was gorgeous. He trailed the tip of his index finger down the V of her breasts, then traced a line just under the lacy edge of her bra cups. Her skin was so soft, so smooth. And he wanted her. Now. 'What time did you say Tanya would be home?'

She shook her head. 'No idea.'

'But it's going to be late?'

'She's going out straight from work so, yes, reasonably late.'

'Good, because I feel an attack of cavemanitis coming on.' He scooped her into his arms, just the way he had on Saturday night when they'd danced together. 'Which is your room?' he asked as he carried her out of the kitchen.

'Top of the stairs, second door on the right.'

He kissed her long and hard and slow, then carried her up the stairs. When he opened the door, he smiled. 'I'm so glad you have a double bed, *estimada*. And lots of pillows.'

'I like to read in bed on a Sunday morning,' she admitted.

He dipped his head slightly to nibble her earlobe. 'I like doing something else. Shall I show you?'

She laughed. 'I thought you'd never ask.'

He set her back down on her feet; she closed the curtains and switched on the bedside lamp, then walked back over to him. 'You need to get out of those wet clothes,' she told him.

'Good plan.' He spread his hands. 'I'll leave it to you, shall I?'

She tugged at the hem of his sweater and he raised his arms, letting her pull the garment over his head. She fanned her fingers over his pectoral muscles. 'Gorgeous,' she breathed.

The feeling was very much mutual, he thought. 'My turn,' he said, and dealt swiftly with her bra before cupping her breasts and rubbing the pads of his thumbs against her hardening nipples. '*Preciósa,*' he murmured. 'So beautiful.'

Her fingers were shaking slightly, he noticed as she undid the buttons of his jeans, and by the time she'd finished, he was shaking, too.

'You're driving me crazy,' he said softly. He stepped out of his jeans, removing his socks as he did so, then finished undressing her.

She ran her hands lightly down his sides. 'You're beautiful.'

He laughed. 'How can a man be beautiful?'

'You are,' she insisted. 'That morning I left you in bed…it was a real wrench to leave. I wanted to kiss all the way down your spine to wake you.'

'I can pretend to be asleep, if you wish. And you can kiss me anywhere you want to wake me.' He moistened his lower lip. 'You've just put some seriously X-rated pictures in my head, so I hope you have protection.'

She shook her head.

He sucked in a breath. Right at that moment he felt as if he was going to implode, he wanted her so much. But he was going to be sensible about this. Do the right thing. 'OK. Is there a late-night chemist or a supermarket nearby?'

'Yes, but you don't have to go there.'

He frowned. 'How so?'

'Because I'm on the Pill. Not for contraceptive purposes,' she explained, 'but because my periods are hideous and this makes them manageable.'

He went very, very still. 'So you're saying you trust me…?'

She nodded.

And this, he knew, was a huge thing for her. Trust. Something he, too, found difficult—and he hadn't yet trusted her with everything in his heart.

Maybe, just maybe, he should try.

'Thank you,' he said softly, and kissed her.

He made love with her very slowly, very tenderly; afterwards, she curled in his arms. 'I could go to sleep now.'

'So could I,' he admitted. Which wouldn't be a good idea, because her housemate was due home. And if he was still here tomorrow morning when Tanya got up, there would be a lot of awkward questions. Questions that would make Becky squirm. 'But I'd better go.' He kissed her lightly, then climbed out of bed and dressed swiftly. When she pushed the covers back, he leaned over to kiss her again. 'I'll see myself out. You stay there.' He stroked her face. 'So are you busy tomorrow?'

'Not exactly—though I do need to catch up on the chores and housework,' she said.

'Then how do you fancy catching a late-afternoon film at the cinema, then have an early meal and go back to my place?' He watched her expression closely. 'And maybe you could stay over. Have breakfast with me before our shift.'

For a moment, he thought she was going to refuse.

And then she smiled. 'That would be lovely.'

'Good. I'll call you tomorrow. Sweet dreams.' He kissed her again, then left the room, pausing at the doorway to blow her a kiss.

Becky lay nestled among the pillows, feeling warm and comfortable, just drowsing and thinking about her gorgeous Catalan lover and how amazing he made her feel. But eventually real life trickled back in and she remembered the washing-up. After their water fight, the kitchen must be in a state. She climbed out of bed, grabbed her dressing-gown and belted it tightly round her waist, then headed downstairs.

And when she reached the kitchen doorway, she stared in amazement.

The washing-up was all done and stacked on the draining-board, and the water on the floor had been mopped up.

She really hadn't expected Leandro to do that.

Michael certainly wouldn't have done it—he would've left the clearing up to her.

So maybe, just maybe, Leandro was different. Maybe you could be completely focused on your career and be a nice guy at the same time, not trample on other people's feelings.

She grabbed her mobile phone from her handbag and sent him a text. *Thank you for clearing up. You didn't have to. And I appreciate it.*

It was a while later that she received a reply: *De res. x*

She smiled.

And she was still smiling the following day when Leandro picked her up and stowed her small overnight bag in the back of his car. Becky couldn't remember the last time she'd gone to the cinema and held someone's hand, but Leandro laced his fingers through hers and it made her feel warm and secure all through the film.

It was definitely starting to feel like a relationship.

Especially when they went for a Chinese meal afterwards, and Leandro opened his fortune cookie. 'Dream your dream, and your dream will dream of you.'

She opened hers. 'Shoot for the moon: if you miss you will still be among the stars.'

'I think they're telling us to have an early night,' Leandro said in a stage whisper, his dark eyes alight with amusement.

'I think,' she whispered back, 'you might be right.'

It felt good to make love with him and fall asleep in his arms. And even better to be woken with a kiss instead of a shrilling alarm the next morning.

And then she noticed the time.

'It's the crack of dawn!' she croaked.

'Not a morning person, *estimada*?' He stroked her face. 'I was thinking we could shower together. Except it might take a while…'

It did. And they were almost late for work.

Luckily nobody seemed to notice that they'd arrived together on the ward on a Sunday morning. They both did the handover with the night staff, Leandro in the main section and Becky in minors, but she'd only seen one patient when Leandro sent Kayleigh to ask her to come to Resus. 'Leandro says we have a

patient coming in with severe hypertension—
he's being sick and he has a bad headache.'

She reached Resus at the same time as the
patient.

Susie, one of the paramedics, brought them up
to speed on the patient's condition. 'Tom Foster,
aged twenty. He was out with his friends last
night—they had a curry and a couple of beers,
but not that many. One of them heard him
throwing up this morning, thought he looked a
bit funny and wondered if he'd got food poisoning, so they called us. His blood pressure's
through the roof. I've already checked with his
mates and none of them do drugs, though they
said Tom's been a bit stressed about his exams.'

'And where are his mates?' Leandro asked.

'Waiting outside.'

'Send them in,' Leandro said. 'We need a chat.'

Becky glanced at the blood-pressure reading
and raised an eyebrow. This was going to be
tough—they needed to get his blood pressure
down again, but if they did it too quickly there
was a risk that Tom would have a stroke or heart
attack, or go into renal failure.

'OK, Tom, I'm Leandro and this is Becky.

We're going to look after you, mate,' Leandro said reassuringly. 'Do you have any heart problems that you know of, or kidney problems?'

Tom's answer was to vomit. 'Oh, God. I'm so sorry,' he moaned.

'Not a problem, honey. We've had much worse in here,' Becky said, squeezing his hand. 'How long have you been feeling like this?'

'Ages. I shouldn't have gone out last night. Should've stayed in and studied.'

'You had a headache last night?' Becky asked.

'A bit.'

She exchanged a glance with Leandro.

'It's difficult to tell the difference between a subarachnoid haemorrhage, a stroke and hypertensive encephalopathy,' Leandro said, 'though I think it might be the latter. Tom, I'm going to shine a penlight into your eyes to check a couple of things, all right? It's not going to hurt and I'll try to be as quick as I can.'

He checked Tom's eyes, and grimaced. 'You've got a couple of haemorrhages in your retina, and your optic disc's a bit swollen—what we call papilloedema. Have you had any problems with your vision lately?'

'No. I just…' Tom doubled over and vomited again, and Becky just about managed to get a bowl in front of him in time.

'So sorry,' he whispered.

'It's all right,' Leandro reassured him. 'Becky, can you check the pulses are all symmetrical and present?'

She did, while Leandro checked the blood pressure in both Tom's arms and listened for bruit. 'No carotid or abdominal or femoral bruit,' he reported, 'and the blood pressure's even.'

'Pulses all symmetrical and present,' Becky confirmed.

'I need urinalysis and urgent bloods,' he said, 'creatinine, sodium and potassium. And get them to do a tox screen while they're at it.' He turned to Tom. 'We're going to hook you up to a machine to see what your heart's doing, and then we're going to send you to the X-ray department—we'll get them to check your chest and do something called a CT scan to see if there's any bleeding into your brain. And we need to take blood samples and a urine sample. Can I have your consent?'

Tom nodded.

'And I think we ought to get in touch with your parents. Do you have their phone number?' Leandro asked.

'Hard to talk,' Tom said. 'Number's…can't remember.'

Becky and Leandro exchanged a glance. Confusion was setting in: that wasn't good. And Tom was clearly finding it hard to breathe.

'We'll give you some oxygen to make things a bit easier. Are you OK with having a mask on?' At the young man's weak nod, she put the mask over his face. 'Nice slow breaths. Take it really easy. That's it, you're doing well.'

The door to Resus opened and two other students came in. 'Is Tom going to be all right?' one of them asked. 'What's wrong with him?'

'We're just trying to rule out a few things,' Leandro said, as Becky started to take the blood samples. 'Look, I'm not going to give you a lecture about anything, and you're not going to get into any trouble at all, but I need to know now in case it affects his treatment—has he taken anything?'

They both shook their heads. 'None of us do drugs. It's a mug's game.'

'You're absolutely sure?' Leandro asked.

'The only thing he's been taking is headache pills—stuff he got from the chemist. He's had a lot of headaches lately,' one of the students said.

'Do you know what he's been taking? Codeine? Paracetamol?'

'Just little white tablets.'

'Any chance you can go back to his room and get us a sample?' Leandro asked.

'It's—well, you don't just go into someone's room and take their stuff,' one of them protested.

'His life could depend on this,' Becky said quietly. 'There are times when it's OK to do it—and this is one of them.'

'All right.'

'And do you have a number for his parents?'

The other student paled. 'Oh, my God. It's that serious?'

'You did the right thing, calling an ambulance,' Leandro said. 'So we need the tablets he's been taking and his parents' number. If you can ring the number through to us…' He scribbled a number on a piece of scrap paper. 'This will get through directly.'

The CT scan ruled out the subarachnoid haemorrhage and the ECG showed no sign of left ventricular failure. Leandro drew up a solution of labelatol with saline while Becky set up a drip.

'Tom, I'm going to put you on a drip—it's putting medication straight into your blood-stream,' he said, 'to help bring your blood pressure down. I'll need to put another needle into you so I can measure your blood pressure continuously and see how you're doing. Is that OK?'

Tom nodded.

'And we need to give you a catheter so we can measure your urine output. It's going to feel a bit uncomfortable, but I promise you'll start feeling a bit better soon.' He turned to Becky. 'We'll start him on this at fifteen mils an hour and then increase it in fifteen minutes—I want him down to about a hundred and ten diastolic,' he said. 'I'm going to put in an arterial line— and I think you should page ICU, as it's the best place to keep an eye on someone with hyperten-sive encephalopathy.'

'Leave it with me,' Becky said.

She was monitoring Tom when the phone rang. 'His parents are in Leeds,' Tom's friend said, and rattled off the number.

Becky read it back to him to check she'd written it down properly, then asked, 'Did you find the tablets?'

'There's two. One's a packet of paracetamol. The other's not marked.'

'Thanks. Can you bring them both in?' Becky asked.

When she'd cleared the line, she rang his parents to explain the situation and they promised to come straight away.

'Before you come—can I just ask you about your family's medical history? Does anyone have blood-pressure problems?'

'No, nobody,' Tom's father said.

'And Tom doesn't take drugs?'

'Of course not. He's a nice boy, though when he went to college we were worried in case he fell in with the wrong crowd and started taking something just to fit in. But his friends are all nice boys, too. They don't do that sort of thing.'

'Sorry to ask. We just had to check. Come to the emergency department and ask for Becky Marston. I'll take you up to him myself,' she said.

Though before Tom's parents arrived, the tox screen was back.

And she knew it wasn't good because Leandro said something very short in his own language.

'Problems?'

'Amphetamines.'

'Oh, no. That's probably what's in the unmarked bottle his friends found. They're bringing in a sample,' Becky explained.

She tried to prepare Tom's parents when she took them up, but neither of them would believe that Tom would have taken drugs. Despite the fact that when the sample arrived, it turned out to be amphetamines.

But at the end of their shift, when Becky and Leandro dropped in to ICU to see how Tom was doing—thankfully, he was going to recover relatively unscathed—the story came out.

'Apparently he's been worried about his exams,' Mrs Foster said ruefully. 'He was worried he wouldn't pass, and ended up so stressed he had a headache. He didn't have any headache tablets, so he borrowed one from someone on his corridor.'

'Except it wasn't a headache tablet,' Mr Foster said. 'It turned out it was speed. It kept Tom awake, and then he hit on the idea that if he took these things he'd be able to stay awake longer and have more time to study. So he's been taking them for a few weeks now.' He sighed. 'He won't tell me the name of the student who gave him the stuff because he doesn't want to get his friend into trouble. But I can't believe he was so stupid.'

'We've told him it doesn't matter how he does in the exams. He doesn't have to be top of the class—we just want him to be happy,' Mrs Foster added.

So different from her own family's reaction, Becky thought. They'd wanted her to be top of the class. To do well. And yet at the same time they'd expected her to give it all up just because Michael had wanted to start a family and they'd thought she should stay at home to raise children.

Happiness hadn't come into it.

'I'm glad he's going to be all right,' she said, forcing a smile to her face.

'We're going to get him some counselling to deal with the stress,' Mrs Foster said. 'Shouting at him isn't going to change what happened. But we want him to know he doesn't have to struggle—that we're there.'

'That's good.' Becky smiled again. 'I better let you get back to your son. Thanks for putting us in the picture.' And she turned away before her mask of composure cracked completely.

CHAPTER NINE

THE expression on Becky's face when the Fosters talked to her about their son haunted Leandro for the next few days. Added to what she'd told him about her family at Alderley Edge, it made him sure that this was why she kept herself at a distance.

So what had happened? Had her ex-husband taken drugs or something, and her parents had taken a dim view of her supporting him?

He didn't get the chance to ask her until the following Sunday, when they'd gone to a special art gallery exhibition featuring Whistler's nocturnes.

'That's how I think of London,' she said, looking at the shadowy monochrome paintings. 'Dark.'

He curled his fingers round hers. 'Because you were unhappy there?'

She nodded.

'Tell me,' he coaxed.

'Not here.' She wrinkled her nose. 'Later.'

They wandered through the rest of the exhibition, and then he found them a quiet table in a corner of a café, somewhere he knew she'd talk to him. Once she'd drunk half her coffee and eaten most of her blueberry muffin, he curled his fingers around hers. 'Talk to me,' he said softly. 'Why was London so bad?'

She grimaced. 'It was like treading on eggshells all the time. One word out of place, and one of my parents would flare up. Half the time I had no idea what they were rowing about—it was like some kind of code.' She shook her head. 'I don't know why they stay together. Well, I do—they don't believe in divorce.'

So if they'd spent a lifetime trapped in a miserable marriage, the fact that their daughter had escaped from one must've gone down really, really badly, Leandro thought. 'They must have loved each other at some point, to get married.'

'Don't you believe it.' Her voice was dry. 'I was about fifteen when I worked it out. My birthday is six months after their wedding anniversary. I was six months old on their first anniversary.' She dragged in a breath. 'And I wasn't premature.'

'It wasn't your fault.'

'But if it hadn't been for me, they wouldn't have got married. They wouldn't have spent all these years being unhappy.'

'First of all, they didn't *have* to get married just because your mother was expecting you. And, secondly, they didn't have to stay together. If a marriage isn't working out, it's clearly better for the child to have one parent and a stable life, knowing they're loved, than to grow up in an atmosphere of constant rowing and believing it's all their fault.'

'That's not the way my parents saw it. They're very traditional.' She sighed. 'And my grandparents even more so.'

He frowned. 'You're, what, twenty-five now?'

'Twenty-seven.'

'If they'd agreed to stay together for your sake, until you left home to do your nursing course, they could've split up nearly ten years ago. So don't blame yourself for them staying together. It was their choice.' He raised her hand to his mouth. 'I'm sorry you had a rough childhood, *estimada*.'

'It's not your fault. And I've learned to live with it.' She shrugged. 'I'm not the only one who had a difficult time. I imagine it wasn't a bed of roses for you either.'

'Growing up in a single-parent family?' He grimaced. 'Although Barcelona likes to think of itself as a happening city, the circles we moved in were very traditional. And my grandparents were the most traditional of the lot.'

'I know exactly where you're coming from,' she said wryly. 'The sort who disapprove of just about everything.'

He remembered what she'd told him about having the grandparents from hell, too. 'Why would they disapprove of you?'

'Let's just say my divorce went down badly. And when they found out the reason why, they came very close to disowning me.'

'So why did you divorce?' He needed to know. 'Did he take drugs?'

She frowned. 'No. What on earth made you think that?'

'Just a feeling I had. You seemed a bit upset about Tom Foster. So I leapt to a few conclusions.' He shrugged. 'Wrong ones.'

'It wasn't anything to do with drugs. It was…' She stopped.

'Tell me,' he said softly.

'It was his parents.' She bit her lip. 'How supportive they were. How the most important thing for them was that he was happy.'

Clearly the complete opposite of the way her parents thought. 'I'm sorry. I take it your parents liked Michael?'

'He was everything they wanted in a son-in-law. But he wasn't the right husband for me.' She sighed. 'We should never have got married in the first place.'

'But you loved him once?'

She nodded. 'Until the shackle went on my finger, everything was fine. But the second I'd signed the marriage register, everything changed. It turned out we didn't want the same things after all. And it got worse and worse and worse—until I stopped loving him and he stopped loving me. And...' She grimaced. 'I'm sorry. I don't normally talk about this.'

'Maybe it will help. Better out than in.'

She shook her head. 'Talking isn't going to change anything. So let's leave it that he wasn't the man I thought he was, and I wasn't the woman he wanted me to be—the woman my parents and grandparents expected me to be.'

'Just for the record,' he said softly, 'I like the woman you are. Very much. On a personal level, you're good company.' Not to mention incredibly sexy and the fact that she made his heart miss a beat every time she smiled at him. 'And on a professional level you're one of the best nurses I've ever worked with.'

'Thank you. Though I wasn't fishing,' she added swiftly.

He smiled. 'I know. But I don't understand why your family aren't shouting from the rooftops how proud they are of you. You're twenty-seven and you're already a nurse practitioner. You're on the senior management team. You've worked hard and done really well—any parent would be delighted at your achievements.'

'It's not the way they are.' She sighed. 'I thought they'd be pleased that I was doing well at work, climbing the career ladder. But, as I said, they're traditional.'

He remembered that look on her face when he'd told her why he was still single. And now he understood what she wasn't telling him. 'You mean, they expected you to give up work when you married?'

She gritted her teeth. 'Give up work and have children.'

He frowned. 'And you don't want children?'

'No. I want to become nurse consultant. Eventually, I want to be nursing director. I want to make a real difference, Leandro. I want to make sure our patients get the best care and our nurses get the best training and support. I want to cut through all the red tape, push the politics aside and make it *happen*.' She paused. 'What about you?'

'My career plan?'

'Do you want children?'

He shook his head. 'Although my mother did a brilliant job of bringing me up, I believe children need two parents around.' At the expression on her face, he added, 'Two parents who work *together* to make the family—if the marriage doesn't work out then, yes, it's better to split up and make sure the children have a stable and happy upbringing. But that's not going to happen for me. I won't be around enough to be a good father, not if I want to make clinical director and maybe professor of medicine. I need to put the hours in.'

'So you'd expect your wife to give up her career and stay home to look after the children?'

'I have no intention of getting married and having children, *estimada*,' he reminded her. 'Is that what your husband expected you to do? Stay home and look after the children?'

Her face was white. 'We didn't have children. But he wanted them. And because he was a doctor and I was only a nurse…it was obvious his career had to come first and mine had to take a back seat.'

'Obvious to whom?'

'Michael. My parents. My grandparents.'

But not Becky herself. He'd worked with her for long enough to know she loved her job and she was good at it—giving it all up would've been a huge wrench. Not to mention unfair. Leandro squeezed her hand. 'There's no such thing as "only" a nurse. Your job is just as valid as a doctor's. You're the one who's there most of the time to look after the patient—and a good experienced nurse will notice if a junior doctor makes the wrong decision, and point it out before it becomes a problem.' He frowned. 'When you meet the man you want to settle down with—' and he refused even to consider that it might be him: they'd agreed this wasn't serious between them, right from the start '—there's no reason why you can't have a career *and* a family, if that's what you want.'

'I don't want children,' she repeated, her face set. 'And every time I go back to London, I have my parents and my grandparents on my case, demanding to know why I was so stupid as to give up a good catch like Michael. A doctor who earned enough to support me so I could stay at home—it didn't occur to them that maybe I didn't want to stay at home, that I didn't want to lose my identity and always be known just as "Michael's wife" or "the children's mother". I wanted to be *me*. Becky. I wanted to do the job I loved and know I'd made a real difference to people's lives. Helped them. And it was my fault he had the affair—if I hadn't been so selfish and given him the children he wanted, he wouldn't have strayed.'

'He had an affair and your family blamed you for it?' He stared at her in disbelief. 'But that's appalling. Of course it wasn't your fault. It was his choice—and the wrong choice by a long, long way. How could they possibly take his side?' His free hand clenched into a fist. 'No decent man would do that to the woman he loves. It wasn't your fault, Becky.'

'But they still had a point. Michael's lover was prepared to give up her career and have children. I wasn't. If I had, maybe he'd have stayed with me instead of going off with her and making her pregnant.'

'But he wouldn't have been worth staying with,' Leandro said. 'There's such a thing as compromise.'

'It didn't happen. There's no point in dwelling on it. And I'm happy with my life as it is. I know what I want and I'm not afraid to go for it—without hurting other people in the process.' She shrugged. 'Anyway, this isn't about me. You were telling me about your family.' She smiled wryly. 'Your grandparents sound like mine. Difficult.'

'We're not close,' Leandro admitted. 'Because my mother decided to keep me and raise me herself, despite not being married, they put her through hell. They disapproved of both of us.' He shrugged. 'But I did well at school and there I noticed that the teachers approved of me. And it struck me that if I worked hard and became a doctor then people in our community would respect me. And if they respected me, then they would also have to respect my mother.'

'So that's why you concentrated on getting promoted as fast as you could?'

'I quickly discovered that I loved my job— but, *sí*, that's what started it all. So my mother could talk about "my son, the consultant" and hold her head up high. To boost her a bit against the gossips and the whisperers. And once she knew what I wanted to do, she worked two jobs to help put me through med school. Secretary by day, cleaner by night.' He felt his mouth tighten. 'My grandparents are quite wealthy.'

Becky frowned. 'Then why didn't they didn't offer to help you through med school?'

'They did.' Bile rose in his throat at the memory. 'On condition that I dissociated myself from my mother.'

'Absolutely *not*.'

The words burst out of her and her eyes

flashed with outrage. He smiled, pleased that she was completely on his wavelength here. 'That's exactly what I said to them. Well, not exactly. I gave them a huge lecture on common decency and I told them I was ashamed of their behaviour—and that I would rather disown *them* as the kind of people I'd never, ever want to be, and my mother had more integrity in the clippings of her little fingernail than they had in their entire bodies.'

'Good for you.'

He smiled. 'Apart from the fact that I love my mother very much—she's one of the kindest, sweetest, most decent people I know—she didn't abandon me when she had the chance. So when I was faced with the same choice, it was very easy for me to make the same decision. To repay her trust in me.'

Leandro was a man of principle, Becky thought. And his childhood certainly explained why he was so driven, why he'd become a consultant so early and let nothing get in his way to the top. 'Does your mother ever talk about your father?' she asked.

'Not until a year or so ago, when she was seriously ill. And she thought she needed to tell me the truth, just in case she…' He stopped and swallowed hard.

She held his hand tighter. 'I'm so sorry.'

'There's nothing to be sorry about.' He smiled wryly. 'My mother is absolutely fine. She recovered from the surgery and she's doing very well. But the truth was out, and once she was better I asked her to tell me more about my father. She wouldn't say much, just that he was an English medical student—which is another reason why my grandparents weren't so happy about my choice of career.'

'Did she tell you his name?'

Leandro nodded. 'So I decided to trace him and talk to him myself, find out why he left my mother.' He rolled his eyes. 'She wasn't talking on that score.'

'You think out of misplaced loyalty to him?'

'*Sí.*' He inclined his head. 'What kind of man walks out on his pregnant girlfriend?'

The kind of man she'd married. Well, he'd gone to his pregnant girlfriend. He'd left his pregnant wife…

She swallowed hard. Michael hadn't known about the baby at the time. Nobody had—even her. Though even if he had known she was pregnant, it wouldn't have stopped him leaving. And it wouldn't have stopped her losing the baby three weeks later. Wouldn't have stopped the guilt crushing her.

The emotions threatened to choke her but she managed to push them back. The longing for the might-have-beens mixed with the gut-wrenching fear that she wouldn't be a good enough mother. The guilt that she'd caused the miscarriage because she hadn't loved the baby.

'Like you said, if a relationship goes wrong, it's better to break it up and give the child a stable and happy upbringing. Maybe,' she said softly, 'your mother realised she would be better off on her own.' Her mother certainly would have been—and Becky was fairly sure her mother might have been a nicer person if she hadn't been tied to Becky's father. If she'd had the chance to meet someone who'd appreciated her for who she'd been, maybe she wouldn't have been disappointed and constantly damping down her anger—or venting it on her daughter.

'No, she wasn't better off on her own. She had to struggle, Becky. It wasn't easy for her at all. And she admitted that if my father had stayed in Barcelona or asked her to go back to England with him, she thought she would have been happy with him,' Leandro said. 'And I believe she's still in love with him, or at least with his memory. Because even though I know for a fact she's been asked out on dates, she's always turned them down.' He grimaced. 'I thought maybe it was because of me. So I asked her. And she just said, no, it wasn't because of me: she just didn't want to settle for second best.'

'Maybe there's more to it than she's told you,' she said.

'You mean, he forgot to tell her that he was already married when he made her pregnant? I thought of that. She says he wasn't. She says he was an honourable man. Though in my book an honourable man doesn't walk out on his pregnant girlfriend. He stays and supports her.' He paused. 'Anyway. I took a chance that he'd qualified and stayed in medicine. There are other doctors with the same name, but this one is the right age. Assuming he didn't lie about to my mother about his age, too.'

Enlightenment dawned. 'And he's here in Manchester? He works at our hospital?'

He nodded. 'You will understand if I don't tell you his name.'

'Yes. Though I hope you know I'd keep your confidence.'

'I know you would.' Leandro's fingers tightened around hers. 'I just need to…'

'Come to terms with it?' she guessed.

'*Sí.* It's strange, growing up and wondering what your father's like. If you're like him at all. If he'd died, that would have been different: people would have talked about him. But because of the way things were, nobody would say anything about him at all, and I knew it hurt my mother to talk about him so I stopped asking.' He shrugged. 'She told me I have his nose, but he had fair hair and blue eyes, and her colouring was genetically the dominant one.'

'I take it you've seen his photograph on the Internet?'

Leandro nodded. 'And I can't see myself in him at all.'

'Have you approached him yet?'

'No. I want to get to know him professionally first. See what kind of man he is. And then maybe I'll talk to him about my mother. Find out what really happened.'

'Sounds like a good plan.' She smiled at him. 'And if you want back-up or support, you know where I am.'

'Thank you. I might take you up on that.' He raised her hand to his mouth and kissed the backs of her fingers. 'You know what I want to do right now?'

'What?'

'Go home with you. Lose myself in you. Forget the demons.'

With her free hand, she reached up and stroked his face. 'Me, too. Thinking about my family always makes me feel like a coiled spring.'

His dark eyes glittered. 'I know a very, very good way of relieving tension. Let's forget the rest of the coffee and go home.'

'That,' she said, 'is the best idea you've had all day.'

CHAPTER TEN

'A LITTLE bird tells me,' Irene said to Becky with a wide grin, 'that you owe me a big box of chocolates.'

'Oh?' Becky tried for nonchalance.

Irene clearly wasn't going to be put off the scent. ''Fess up. You and Leandro are an item, aren't you? And don't give me any of that stuff about seeing each other outside work to talk about departmental stuff. You can do that in the hospital canteen—you don't have to go all the way to Alderley Edge to do it.'

Becky smiled ruefully. 'We *were* talking departmental stuff, actually.'

'Right. And that was what you were doing, walking hand in hand through the city centre, the other day?' Irene raised an eyebrow.

Obviously they'd been spotted. Well, she should've known that the hospital grapevine wouldn't miss a thing. Becky sighed. 'All right. I owe you chocolates.'

'So you admit he's the most gorgeous man you've ever seen?'

Becky squirmed.

'That wouldn't be me you're talking about?' a deep voice queried, full of laughter.

Irene blushed spectacularly. 'Um…'

Leandro came to stand beside Becky and looped his arm round her shoulders. 'Yes, Irene, we're seeing each other outside work. But as far as we're both concerned, our patients come first and, regardless of what happens outside the department, inside we're a team and we just work together. OK?'

'OK.'

'Good.' He smiled at her. 'And I'll buy you the chocolates myself.'

'I was only having a bit of a laugh,' Irene said. 'I didn't mean…'

'Yes, you did. You're the department's biggest chocoholic,' Becky teased back. 'Any excuse. But, as Leandro said, we're keeping this low key. We're just good friends.'

'With a little something extra,' Leandro whispered in her ear, his voice low enough so that only she would hear, making a shiver of delight ripple down her spine.

'Just good friends,' Irene scoffed. 'Right, and I'm a supermodel.' She smiled. 'Actually, I think you two might be good for each other.'

'Thank you,' Leandro said. 'Just as long as you remember, at work, we're strictly colleagues. And I'd really prefer to avoid gossip.'

The fact that Leandro and Becky worked well together as a team showed later that day when a patient came in with a fever, headache and stiffness in her neck.

'I thought it was just a bug, but you see all that stuff about meningitis. And I can't move my neck. And they say the rash doesn't always appear,' she said to Becky. 'I was going to leave it, but my son said I ought to come in and get checked over.'

'Let's have a look at you, Mrs Emerson,' Becky said gently. 'When did you first start feeling bad?'

'About a month ago. I thought it was flu and now it's come back. Except you don't have a stiff neck and back pain with flu, do you?'

'Can you describe the pain for me?' Becky asked.

'It's here, between my shoulder blades and my neck.'

'Does it get better or worse if you do anything in particular?'

'It's worse at night,' Mrs Emerson said, 'when I'm lying down.'

'Anything else you've noticed?'

Mrs Emerson bit her lip. 'My face is a bit numb.'

'And have you noticed any kind of rash or sensitive bits on your skin?'

'No.'

There was a pattern emerging here, but Becky wanted a second opinion. 'I'm just going to call one of the doctors to come and talk to you,' she said gently.

'Is it something serious?'

'Try not to worry,' Becky said, squeezing her hand. 'I don't think it's meningitis, so you can relax on that score, but I'm just wondering…have you been walking a lot lately?'

'Yes. We had a walking holiday in the States. Last month.'

The picture was getting clearer. 'Do you know

if you were bitten by any kind of insects? Or had a reaction to, say, poison ivy?'

'I had a couple of tick bites,' Mrs Emerson admitted, 'but these things happen when you're on a walking tour. I've been bitten by ticks before and not had a problem. And I'm sure I got it off without squeezing its head so I couldn't have caught anything nasty.'

Becky wasn't quite so sure. 'Thank you. I'll be back in a moment, Mrs Emerson.'

The first doctor she came across when she left the cubicle was Leandro. 'Just the man I wanted,' she said.

He laughed. 'Now, there's a thought. What can I do for you?'

'Second opinion,' she said, and filled him in on her patient's symptoms. 'But the only thing that's odd is that she doesn't have a rash.'

'You're thinking complications of Lyme disease?' he asked.

'Yes. But without the rash, the presentation isn't quite right. I wonder if it's some sort of neuro thing.'

'There isn't always a rash—and it could be neuro borrelia. I'll come and have a chat with her.' He followed Becky into the cubicle.

'Mrs Emerson, this is Mr Herrera, our consultant.' Becky introduced him swiftly.

'Mrs Emerson, would you mind answering a few questions for me, please?' Leandro's smile was reassuring and charming, and Mrs Emerson visibly relaxed.

'Of course.'

'From what Becky tells me of your symptoms, I agree that it sounds very much like a complication of Lyme disease—something we call neuro borrelia.'

'But I wasn't ill after I got the tick off.'

'Sometimes it takes a while to show up. You can get several diseases from ticks,' he said gently. 'Lyme disease is the most common, and it's a caused by a bacterium called *Borrelia burgdorferi* which is transmitted from the bite of an infected tick. Not all ticks are infected, so you're right, it's perfectly possible to be bitten by a tick and not have any problems. After you were bitten, can you remember having any sort of rash?'

'No.'

'With Lyme disease, you often get a rash with a clear centre, and it tends to move about a bit over the body. Though it isn't always obvious—

sometimes it's just red and blotchy and it's easy to confuse it with a poison ivy rash.'

'So if I don't have a rash, I don't have Lyme disease.'

'The rest of your symptoms are typical, but I need to do some tests to find out what the problem is. I need to do a blood test and also to take a little tiny bit of fluid from your spinal cord. And I'd like to send you for a CT scan of your nervous system—that's a special kind of X-ray and nothing to worry about.'

'Am I going to be OK?'

'Yes, but the treatment does take time. I'm going to put you on antibiotics and have a chat with the infectious diseases specialist.'

'Infectious? Is my family going to be affected?'

'In all likelihood, no. But if you've been walking around with this for a few weeks, I'm very glad you came in now. If you'd left it much longer it might have caused you some problems,' Leandro said seriously. 'But don't worry, we can help. And I'm very good with needles—you ask Becky.'

'The best,' she said with a smile.

'Is it going to hurt? Not the blood test, I've had that before. The other thing.'

'The lumbar puncture. It sounds much scarier than it is,' Leandro said. 'I'm going to put a local anaesthetic in the area so it shouldn't hurt.'

'And I'll be here to hold your hand all the way through it,' Becky promised. 'What we'd like you to do is lie on your side and I'll put a pillow between your knees to support your upper leg and stop you rolling forward—that will put you in the right position for the procedure.'

'Oh, dear.' Mrs Emerson's lower lip wobbled. 'I wish I'd asked my husband to come home from work.'

'I can call him any time you like,' Becky said. 'But the sooner we get these samples to the lab, the sooner we can give you the right treatment.'

Mrs Emerson sighed. 'He'll be in a meeting anyway.'

'I promise we'll make this as quick and painless as possible,' Leandro said.

Becky got the spinal needle ready, along with three plain bottles and a fluoride bottle. Between them, she and Leandro guided Mrs Emerson in the right position, talking to her and reassuring her all the while. Finally Mrs Emerson's back was vertical and right to the edge of the bed. 'Now, if you can keep your shoulders nice and square for me…' Leandro said softly.

'I'll try.' Mrs Emerson screwed her face up, obviously expecting it to hurt, and Becky held her hand.

'It's going to be fine,' she soothed.

'Count backwards for me,' Leandro said, 'from fifty-nine. In sevens.'

'Sevens?' Mrs Emerson queried, but did so.

Becky hid her smile. She was getting used to Leandro's distraction techniques—and they worked.

He stretched Mrs Emerson's skin between his thumb and forefinger and inserted the lignocaine. 'That should numb you nicely,' he said.

Mrs Emerson blinked. 'You've done it already?'

'The local anaesthetic, yes.'

'Told you he was good with needles,' Becky said.

Swiftly, Leandro inserted the spinal needle, took the samples, removed the needle again and put a dressing over the wound. 'I'm going to admit you,' he said, 'as I'd like you to see the specialist.'

'So it might not be Lyme disease?' Mrs Emerson asked hopefully.

'It's neuro borrelia,' Leandro said. 'The samples are just going to confirm it. But the good news is that we can treat it.'

'Do I have to stay in?'

'I'm afraid so,' Leandro said.

'I'll take you up to the ward,' Becky said, 'and introduce you to the nurse who'll be looking after you. And I'll call your husband to let him know what's going on and where he can find you.'

She sorted out the admission, settled Mrs Emerson in, and reassured her husband before heading back down to the emergency department.

Odd. They were so in tune at work, it felt as if she'd worked with Leandro for years. And they were in tune outside, too.

She couldn't ever remember being this happy, even in the early days with Michael. She just had to remind herself that it wasn't going to last—that Leandro would be going back to Barcelona, and that would be the end.

She was just going to make the most of the

time they had together. Enjoy it. Store up some good memories to keep her smiling through the tough times.

While she was doing paperwork one afternoon, her computer pinged, telling her an instant message had come through. She glanced at the screen and saw the message was from Leandro.

Tempted as she was to flick into the message screen and read what he had to say, the paperwork had to come first. They were at work.

Another ping. Leandro again.

She gave in and read the message.

I know you're there. Hello?

Busy doing paperwork, she tapped in.

Me, too. Are you busy this evening? came back almost immediately.

No. Why?

It's my fencing evening. Want to come with me tonight?

And see him as a buccaneer? She smiled, then sobered quickly as a thought struck her. *Just to watch, yes? Not to wave a sword about myself?*

His reply was a smiley face.

Followed swiftly by, *Up to you. If you want to*

have a try, the club can lend you the gear. Or bring a book in case you get bored watching. I'll buy you dinner afterwards.

You're on, she typed. *And you have as much paperwork to do as I have, so stop slacking and distracting the staff.*

Sí, senyora, was the response.

She frowned. *Aren't you supposed to have a tilde over the n?*

Spanish, yes; Catalan, no. I'll give you another lesson tonight. Today's verb is fer l'amor.

She had to look that up; and it made her smile. 'To make love.' *Indeed, Mr Herrera. See you later.*

That evening, she didn't need a book—she was mesmerised by Leandro. Even though he was wearing the same outfit as everyone else— a white padded jacket and breeches, a mask to protect his face, white shoes with good grips and a metallic vest which he'd explained to her registered the touch of his opponent's weapon— she could tell him apart from the others.

And he looked magnificent.

She'd teased him about being a musketeer, but the way he moved—wielding his foil with such delicate and swift precision, so graceful light on his feet—stunned her. She couldn't take her eyes off him. Although she knew every muscle, every sinew, every inch of skin, this was a part of him she hadn't seen before. And he was utterly gorgeous.

No wonder he was such a good dancer, too. He was utterly in tune with his body.

And utterly in tune with hers.

After Leandro had showered and changed back into his normal clothes following the fencing bout, he slid his arm round her shoulders and kissed her cheek. 'Sorry for keeping you waiting, Becky. Were you horribly bored?'

'No. I loved watching you,' she admitted. 'It looked almost like...well...ballet.'

'Dancing and fencing have a few things in common,' he said with a smile.

'The main one being that it looks easy and delicate from the outside, but if you try it yourself it's a lot harder and your muscles ache the next morning in places you never even knew existed?'

He laughed. 'Something like that. Come on.

I'm starving.' He brushed his mouth against hers. 'For food. And definitely for you.'

On the team night out at a salsa club in the middle of Manchester, Becky's colleagues made it clear they'd noticed the relationship—and approved.

'You're so lucky,' Kayleigh sighed when Leandro had gone to fetch Becky a drink. 'If you weren't so nice to work with, I'd have to hate you. He's *gorgeous*. And, man, can he dance.'

Becky smiled. 'You know Latino men—they're born with an inbuilt sense of rhythm that Englishmen have to really work for.'

'It's not just that. It's…' Kayleigh sighed. 'Oh, everything. And every single female in the hospital thinks the same. He's gorgeous. Sex on legs. But he doesn't act as if he knows it. And he treats all the staff with respect, doesn't look down on the nurses or the auxiliaries. You're so *lucky*, Becky.'

Becky didn't disabuse her colleague by telling her that it was a temporary fling—the arrangement she'd made with Leandro was just between the two of them. And if Leandro overheard any part of the conversation, he didn't bring it up when they were back at his house. But he made love to her slowly that night, so tenderly that she could've cried.

It was a long, long time since she'd been this happy.

And nothing, but nothing, was going to spoil it.

CHAPTER ELEVEN

A FEW weeks later, Becky was feeling decidedly off colour. She couldn't face her usual cup of coffee in her morning break; instead, she sipped cold water. And even that didn't help much.

Maybe it was a bug, she thought as she wrote up her notes. Not that she was aware of anything doing the rounds. And she definitely hadn't eaten anything that had disagreed with her—she'd eaten either in the hospital canteen or with Leandro, and her colleagues were all perfectly well.

And then a seriously nasty thought hit her.

The last time she'd felt like this…

No. She *couldn't* be pregnant. She was on the Pill, and she'd always taken it properly. And she hadn't had a stomach upset or taken antibiotics for any reason so there was no way the contraceptive could have been affected. Besides, she'd had a period last month, hadn't she?

A very light one.

A chill ran down her spine.

No, she was just being paranoid.

But she took her diary from her handbag anyway. Skimmed through the pages, looking for the little red dot.

Six weeks ago.

No.

Absolutely no way could she be this late.

But the evidence stared her in the face.

And there had been that Saturday night she'd spent at Leandro's when she'd forgotten to take her pills with her and had thought everything would be fine as long as she took the one she'd missed when she went back to her own house on the Sunday.

Had she taken it?

She couldn't remember. Worst-case scenario, if she'd been really stupid and forgotten… She flicked through her diary to that weekend and the sick feeling intensified. The missing pill had been smack in the middle of her cycle. So if the contraceptive had failed…

No.

She couldn't be pregnant.

Please, let her be going down with something.

Please, don't let her be pregnant.

She tried to concentrate on her paperwork, but all she could think of was the fact that she might be pregnant.

No way was she going to do a pregnancy test at work. If the hospital grapevine caught even the faintest idea of this, her life would be hell.

Three hours until the end of her shift.

She'd go home the long way round. Via a supermarket she didn't normally use. A place where nobody was likely to recognise her or spot what was in her shopping basket.

It took her ages to sort out the paperwork, because she had such a hard job concentrating. And she was taken by surprise by the rap on her office door.

'Are you all right?' Leandro asked.

'I'm fine,' she snapped. Lying through her teeth.

He raised an eyebrow. 'You don't sound it. And you don't look it either.'

Oh, lord. She had to do some damage limitation here. The last thing she needed right now was him guessing what was really wrong. Because she remembered all too clearly what he'd said to her. *I have no intention of getting married and having children.* His career would come first.

Like Michael and yet not like Michael—because her ex-husband had, after all, wanted children.

But Leandro was more ambitious. More focused on his career—driven, even. He'd told her his career plans—he wanted to be the clinical director of a hospital, a professor of medicine. To get to the top. And that meant he didn't have room in his life for a wife and children.

He wouldn't want this baby.

She grimaced and rubbed her temples. 'Sorry. I didn't mean to bite your head off. I'm trying to concentrate on this paperwork and I've got a bit of a headache.'

So far, so true. She just wasn't telling him the rest of it. That deep inside she was panicking. Panicking that she was pregnant again and her career was going to go down the tubes and she'd lose everything she'd worked so hard for—and yet at the same time panicking that she might miscarry again, feel the little life seeping out of her the way it had last time. Panicking that if she

did have the baby she'd be a hopeless mother—
that she'd resent her child for taking away her
career and take out her disappointment on the
baby, the way her own mother had taken her dis-
appointments out on her.

Everything was so mixed up, she didn't know
what to think any more.

And she couldn't stop this horrible feeling of
dread, the way her heart was racing and the back
of her neck felt hot and bile was rising in her throat
and she had that horrible humiliating sensation
that she was about to lose control of her bladder.

'A headache, hmm? I can do something about
that.' Before she realised Leandro's intentions,
he sat down on the chair next to hers, and spun
her chair round so that she was facing away
from him. 'Lean backwards,' he directed.

'Leandro…'

'Just try it,' he said softly. 'You know as well
as I do that a scalp massage is the best way to
increase blood flow to the brain—and that's the
quickest way to get rid of a headache.'

His hands were so sure, so gentle. And Becky
wanted to bawl her eyes out.

'You're all tense,' Leandro commented.

That was the understatement of the century. But she needed to calm down—right now she was building bridges to trouble and it wasn't helping at all.

'I'm just feeling a bit off colour,' she muttered, sitting up and pulling away from his gentle hands.

'Maybe you're coming down with something,' he said. 'Look, you're practically at the end of your shift. Have you done the handover?'

She nodded.

'Then go home. And don't look at me like that—you know as well as I do that you tend to stay beyond the end of your shift so you've more than made up your hours already. Leaving early because you're feeling unwell is the sensible thing to do, is it not?'

'I'll probably be all right by the time I've walked home—once I've had a bit of fresh air to clear my head.'

'You're not well. I'll drive you.'

'Apart from the fact that you're still on duty and have patients who need you, walking will be better for me,' she protested. 'Look, I'll have a cup of tea and a couple of paracetamol when

I get home, then go to bed. A nap will probably help. And an early night.'

He looked searchingly at her, then finally nodded. 'OK. I won't ring you later in case you're asleep and I disturb you—but if you need me, you know my number.'

'Thank you.'

To her horror, he leaned forward and kissed her gently on the temple. So tenderly that it made her want to cry.

For the first time in a long, long while, she was actually glad to leave work. If she had to wait much longer to find out the truth, she'd turn into a basket case.

She walked home, via a supermarket she didn't usually visit. Checked over her shoulder before she put a pregnancy testing kit in her shopping basket. Covered it with a box of tissues in case she bumped into anyone she knew. And then rushed her package home.

'One blue line. That's what you're going to tell me, OK?' she informed the little white stick. 'One line. Not pregnant.'

Please. She liked her life just the way it was. She didn't want everything to change. Not now.

The single minute it took to get the result felt like hours. Every second dragged. And with each tick of the clock she was reminded of the last time she'd done this. When she'd waited for the results, holding the test stick and she could still see the pale line of skin and slight indentation where her wedding ring had been. When her life had been shattered into tiny little pieces. All the anger and the fear and the guilt and the worry churning round inside.

Last time she'd taken a pregnancy test, she'd been newly separated—not divorced but well on the way because Michael had gone to live with his pregnant girlfriend. She'd been horrified to discover that she was pregnant, and she'd known straight away that she'd have to bring the baby up on her own. That she'd get no support from Michael, no support from her family.

This time she was also single. In a relationship that had a strict time limit. Would a pregnancy change that? Would Leandro want to make their relationship permanent? Or would he walk away? Would she be on her own again, have to be the one to make all the sacrifices for the baby's sake? On the one hand he'd said that no honourable man would walk out on his pregnant girlfriend; on the other he'd been adamant that he didn't want children. So how would he react when she told him?

What scared her was that she didn't know. She couldn't even begin to guess his reaction.

What scared her even more was that she didn't know how she felt about it either. A baby would be the end of her career plans. And yet…when she'd lost the baby last time, she'd cried herself to sleep for months. Even though her head had known it had probably all been for the best, the pain had been deeper even than the hurt Michael had caused her. And she was always very aware of the day that would have been the baby's birthday. Wondered what her child would be like now.

She'd told Leandro she didn't want children.

But had that been the truth?

Right now, she didn't know any more.

She glanced at her watch. One minute. Taking a deep breath, she checked the test stick. And she stared at it in dismay when she realised there were no blue lines at all.

The test hadn't worked.

'Oh, for pity's sake,' she said in exasperation.

Just as well she'd bought a double pack. She drank a glass of water, then waited half an hour before redoing the test—thirty minutes in which she failed to read more than three consecutive words in a paragraph of the newspaper, did all of two clues in a crossword, paced the floor countless times, and finally stomped off to the bathroom.

This time, the test *had* to work. And it was going to be negative. If she wished hard enough, it would be negative. And that would give her time to think about things—time to think about what she really wanted from her life.

Sixty seconds ticking through treacle.

One blue line.

She sagged in relief. Negative.

She put the test stick on the bathroom window and splashed her face with water. Thank heaven. She wasn't pregnant. Life could go on exactly the way it was. Still working towards a promotion and still seeing Leandro, but knowing there was a time limit and her heart wasn't going to get broken.

Everything was fine.

She dried her face, glanced at the test stick again for reassurance—and promptly dropped the towel.

Since when had that second line been there?

Or maybe she'd counted wrongly. Rushed through the seconds in her head instead of counting them properly against the clock.

She closed her eyes, just in case she was so light-headed with relief at not being pregnant that she was hallucinating. Then she took a deep breath and looked again.

Two blue lines.

Oh, lord.

She sat down on the floor, drew her knees up to her chin and wrapped her arms around her legs.

She was pregnant.

With Leandro's baby.

What on earth was she going to do?

She sat curled up like that for a while, rocking gently, too shocked for tears to come. And then she pulled herself together. Tanya was on an early shift, which meant she'd be back soon; Becky didn't want her housemate worrying about her. And she also didn't want to discuss what was wrong. She needed time to get her head around the idea before she talked to anyone about it—and when she did talk, she knew that the first person she really ought to tell was Leandro.

Swiftly, she wrapped the two tests and their packaging in a carrier bag, wrapped that bag inside another one, and stuffed it at the bottom of the dustbin. She scribbled a quick note to Tanya, saying that she was coming down with a bug so she'd gone to bed with some hot lemon—it wasn't true, but it would give her the space she needed to think.

And tomorrow she was going to have to tell Leandro.

CHAPTER TWELVE

LEANDRO didn't catch up with Becky until nearly lunchtime. And she looked terrible. There were huge shadows under her eyes, and she was much paler than usual.

'Come on, you. Fresh air and a sandwich in the park,' he decreed.

'I'm not—'

'I don't care if you're not hungry. You need to eat to keep your blood-sugar levels stable. And you look terrible. Are you sure you should even be at work right now?'

'Of course I should.'

'Hmm.' He wasn't convinced. He shepherded her down to the canteen, made her choose a sandwich, some fruit and a bottle of water, and then walked with her to the little park opposite the hospital.

'I'm not going to ask you if you're feeling better,' he said as he spread his jacket on the grass and indicated to her to sit down, 'because you don't look it.'

'I'm fine.'

A barefaced lie if ever he'd heard one. But, then again, all the medics he knew loathed being under the weather and would do almost anything to prove they weren't ill.

But when she'd just sat there for ten minutes, staring into space and crumbling her sandwich into the little plastic container and not saying a single word to him, he sighed.

'All right. Spit it out.'

'What?'

'Whatever's on your mind. And, please, don't try to tell me there's nothing wrong. You're never normally this quiet.'

She took a deep breath. 'There isn't a good time or a place to say this.'

This didn't bode well. Ice trickled down his spine. 'Say what?'

'I'm pregnant.'

He stared at her, not quite sure he'd heard her correctly. 'Run that by me again.'

This time, she looked him in the eye. 'I'm pregnant.'

He felt his eyes narrow. 'How?'

'You're a doctor. You know how reproduction works.'

Her sarcastic tone made him snap back. 'That isn't what I meant, and you know it. I thought you were on the Pill?'

'I am.'

'Then how…?'

She stared at him, looking outraged. 'I haven't done this on purpose, you know!'

'I wasn't claiming that you had,' he said coolly.

'I must've missed a pill or taken it late or something. I don't know.'

His first reaction was shock. How could she have been so *careless*?

Then he felt mean. It wasn't fair to blame her. It took two to make a baby. He was just as much at fault—he should've insisted on using a condom despite the fact that she was on the Pill, making absolutely sure something like this wouldn't happen.

He raked a hand through his hair. '*Deu*, Becky. I wasn't expecting this.'

It changed everything.

So much for their casual affair. The one with the time limit. The one where they'd both known what they were doing.

Now she was pregnant.

Expecting his baby.

He was going to be a father.

So much for his plans. Because he couldn't leave her now, could he? Robert Cordell had walked out on Leandro's mother when she was pregnant—he'd never even seen his infant son. Leandro wasn't going to do that. He wasn't the kind of man who'd walk out on his pregnant girlfriend and leave her to deal with everything on her own.

But equally he'd never, ever seen himself as a husband. A father. His job had always come first—he didn't have room in his life for a family as well as his career.

Then again, Becky had big plans for her career, too. She wanted to be nursing director. And she'd said that she didn't want children either. So he imagined that the news was just as much of a shock to her as it was to him.

He felt as if the world had just shifted on its

axis. Changed direction. He didn't know where he was heading any more.

'Are you sure you're pregnant?' he asked. Just to check this wasn't some incredibly realistic nightmare.

'The tests are accurate nowadays.'

He dragged in a breath. 'How long?'

She shook her head. 'I don't know. I only found out myself last night.'

'You said you felt ill.'

'I did. But it wasn't what I thought it was. And it wasn't until I checked my diary that I realised my period was late.'

He didn't buy that. Not at all. 'You must have had some idea, to make you do the test.'

Yes. Previous experience.

Not that she was going to share that with him.

'I was ruling out possibilities.'

'I see. So how late are you?'

His voice was so calm, so controlled. This wasn't the teasing lover who took her to the edge of paradise. He was a complete stranger. One whose mind she couldn't even begin to read. 'My last period was six weeks ago.'

'So you're two weeks late. It's early days.'

Becky stared at him in shock. 'Are you saying you're expecting me to have a termination?'

He frowned. 'No. Of course not.'

'Then why did you say it?'

'I was trying to work out when the baby was due.' He paused. 'Are you telling me you want to have a termination?'

'No.' To her horror, her voice came out as a croak. And her eyes were stinging. She blinked hard, willing the tears to stay back. She wasn't going to cry. Wasn't going to let herself remember. Wasn't…

Too late.

His thumb brushed away the single tear that had escaped and was trickling down her cheek. And then he sighed and hauled her onto his lap.

'Ah, Becky. It's going to be all right,' he said softly, stroking her hair.

Hating herself for being weak, she still couldn't stop herself resting her cheek against his shoulder. 'How? This changes everything. You don't want children.'

'Neither do you.'

'I can't…I can't have a termination. I just *can't.*'

'Nobody's saying you have to.'

Just as well, because she didn't want to drag up all the misery. 'Then what are you suggesting?' How could he possibly make things all right again?

'You're moving in with me—and we're getting married just as soon as I can arrange a licence.'

Marriage.

That was where everything had gone wrong with Michael.

And how did she know it wouldn't be the same with Leandro? How did she know that he wouldn't resent her and the baby for holding him back? As it was, he tended to be in early and stay late so even if they did get married, his priority would be his work. He'd hate being dragged home early.

But the clincher was the fact he'd said he'd marry her out of duty. Not because he loved her. She knew he didn't want a wife or children so this wouldn't be a proper marriage. And she wasn't going to settle for anything less than love. Someone who loved her with all his heart, who'd love their baby, too.

'No. No way.'

He frowned, and moved her slightly so he

could look into his face. 'Becky, I know we both said we don't want children. But these things happen. I will do the right thing by you—I'll give you and the baby my name.'

So she had the proof without even asking for it. He didn't love her. He wasn't going to be delighted at the idea of being a father once he'd had time to get over the initial shock. He was simply doing what he saw as his duty.

Which wasn't what she wanted. At all.

'That's what happened to my parents. They got married because of me. And I had a *really* miserable childhood—they resented each other and they resented me and I couldn't wait to leave home. I'm not letting *my* child go through that.'

His frown deepened. 'I grew up illegitimate. I know what the stigma is like. And I'm not going to let my child go through that.'

'Apart from the fact that you were born thirty-five years ago and times have changed, England isn't the same as Spain. Catalonia,' she amended quickly, when his eyes narrowed. 'It's different nowadays.'

'No, it isn't.'

'Yes, it is,' she countered. 'I'm not getting married to you for all the wrong reasons. I've been married before.'

'And I'm nothing like your first husband.'

'Yes, you are. He's ambitious. So are you. His career came first. So will yours.'

He sighed. 'Look, we're both going to have to adjust. Make compromises.'

'And you'll resent me for that. You'll resent the baby for that. And I'm not going to let that happen.'

'So what are you suggesting? That you're going to be a single mother?'

'It worked for your mother. You've turned out OK.'

He shook his head. 'I spent the first thirty-five years of my life never knowing my father. I always had the feeling that something was missing in my life, that it made me different from my friends.'

'And I spent *my* childhood knowing that I was different because my friends' parents didn't fight all the time—their parents hadn't married just to give the baby a surname. Getting married isn't always the right thing to do.'

'Agreed, if it's for the wrong reason.'

'And marrying me to give the baby your name is definitely the wrong reason.'

Leandro couldn't argue with that. 'So you're saying you'll only get married for love.'

'Yes.'

Did he love Becky?

He'd avoided thinking about it. But now he was forced to face it, and he realised that his feelings towards her over the last few weeks had changed. He still felt that overpowering rush of desire every time he saw her—but there was something else, too. Something more.

He'd told himself it was because he liked her. Respected her as a colleague and enjoyed her company.

But it wasn't that at all.

It was something he'd never, ever felt before. Becky Marston was the only woman who'd ever made him feel this way. And the adrenaline rush of working in the emergency department wasn't the only reason he looked forward to work any more—it was because Becky would be there, working by his side. Or if she was in minors while he was in clinic then he always knew he'd see her at the end of their shift.

Love.

He'd never, ever thought the day would happen when he'd fall in love.

But it had.

He was in love with Becky. And the realisation completely sideswiped him.

Then he became aware that she was waiting for him to speak. Clearly she'd said something and he'd been so lost in his thoughts he hadn't heard her. '*Em sap greu.* I wasn't listening. What did you say?'

'I said I can't marry you, Leandro.'

His mind made the leap. She'd just told him he'd only marry for love. And she'd just said she wouldn't marry him. Which meant she didn't love him.

Before he could protest—say that maybe she could learn to love him, that they needed to give this a try for their unborn child's sake—she'd wriggled off his lap. Stood up.

'I'm sorry, Leandro. It isn't going to work. And this thing between you and me…we need to stop.'

She was ending it? *Now*? When she'd told

him she was expecting his baby? He stared at her, too shocked to speak.

'I think it's best if we're strictly colleagues from now on.'

That galvanised him into speech. 'Hang on. Things have changed. It isn't like it was in the beginning. You're pregnant with my child.'

'You don't want children.'

'I'm not walking out on you.'

'No. *I'm* walking out on *you*. So your conscience is clear.'

He stood up, but she moved out of reach before he could take her hand.

'I need to go back to work. I'll be late.'

'This isn't over, Becky,' he warned her.

'Yes, it is.'

'We need to talk about this. Decide what we're going to do. And decide it together.'

She shook her head. 'You've made it pretty clear how you feel.'

'No, I haven't. Don't be so unreasonable! You've just turned my world upside down and I can't think straight enough even to begin to know how I feel, let alone try to guess what you want from me. And I'd bet you're in the same state as I am. You're shocked and you're suddenly having to consider something you've never even thought about before.'

That was where he was wrong. This was something she'd had to think about once before. But she couldn't bring herself to tell him. How her periods had stopped when Michael had left and she'd thought it was just stress—and then she'd started being sick. She'd taken a pregnancy test just to prove to herself that it was stress…and had discovered that it wasn't. That she had been expecting a baby.

Days and days of thinking it over. Wondering what she was going to do. Worrying that she'd be no good as a mother. Worrying that she wouldn't be able to juggle her job and the baby. Convinced that she was going to make a huge mess of everything and then Michael would demand custody and take the baby away from her.

And then, just when she'd adjusted to the idea of being a mother, discovering that she wasn't going to be one after all. The pain had been incredible. The aching emptiness of loss—quickly filled by guilt. The baby had known she hadn't wanted it at first, and that was why she'd lost it.

Her deepest, darkest, nastiest secret. One that she'd never shared with anyone.

'I'm going back to work,' she said, as coolly as she could. 'And I'd appreciate it if you gave me some space.'

'Becky—'

But she was already walking away.

Luckily they were so busy in the unit that afternoon she didn't have time to think about her personal circumstances.

But when she was nearing the end of her paperwork, there was a knock on her open door. She looked up, and caught her breath when she saw Leandro.

'Can I come in?'

She could hardly say no. Not without giving the rumour mill something to talk about. 'Whatever.'

He closed the door behind him. 'Becky. We really need to talk.'

'There's nothing to talk about.'

'Yes, there is. We're going to have a baby.'

'I'm going to have a baby,' she corrected. 'You have nothing to worry about. You've done the right thing. You offered to marry me, and I refused. So your conscience is clear and you can leave me to get on with it. And my paperwork,' she added. 'I'm busy.'

'I can't do that.'

She lifted her chin. 'I'm sure you don't want to embarrass us both by making me call Security.'

His eyes widened. 'Becky. Don't be like this.'

'Like what? We're just colleagues from now on. It's over.'

'No.' He shook his head. 'It's not over. Not by a long way. And it's not just you and me any more. It's the baby as well.'

'It's not your problem.'

'I grew up,' he said softly, 'not knowing my father. And I'm not letting that happen to my child.' His gaze was level. 'This isn't over. And you're going to talk to me. Whether you like it or not.'

Did that mean he was going to insist on custody? Despite the fact that he'd be living in a different country? The lump in her throat grew bigger. 'I need space, Leandro. I need time to think, to work things out. Don't make this any harder for me than it already is.'

'Time.' The silence stretched between them, then finally he nodded. 'All right. I'll give you a week. But then we talk—and I mean *really* talk.'

As far as she was concerned, there was nothing more to say. But if she argued with him now, he'd push and push and push until she told him everything. And she was close enough to tears as it was. If she let any of this out, she'd be a crumbling wreck. 'A week,' she whispered.

'One week.' He turned to go, then paused at the door. 'If you want to talk sooner, you know my number. And I want you staying clear of X-rays or anything dangerous, do you under-stand? No risk-taking.'

And this time, when the door closed behind him, she really had to wipe the tears away.

She just had to be strong. For her own sake as well as the baby's. Because she wasn't going to end up in another marriage that was doomed to failure before it began.

CHAPTER THIRTEEN

LEANDRO spent a sleepless night. Missing Becky. Thinking about her. Thinking about the news that had completely shaken both their worlds.

She was having his baby.

He'd offered to marry her.

And she'd refused. Said she would only marry for love.

Hmm.

So had she refused his proposal because she didn't love him, or had she refused because she thought he didn't love her?

He'd never told her he loved her.

Just as she'd never told him.

But the way it was between them when they made love…it was like nothing else he'd known. Deeper. More fulfilling. Because he loved her. And he was sure he wasn't alone in that feeling—that it was the same for her.

Maybe he should call her. Tell her how he felt.

But he'd promised her a week. Time to get used to what was happening between them. If he pushed her too hard now, he'd lose her for ever.

On the other hand, if he left it a whole week it'd give her time to shore up her defences and build a huge wall round herself.

He paced the house. This was so stupid. At work he never had problems making a decision. He knew exactly what he was doing, and even when the unexpected happened he dealt with it, calmly and kindly and efficiently. He'd never dithered in his personal life before either.

So why the hell was he dithering now?

He sighed, already aware of the answer. Because he had too much to lose. He loved Becky: for the first time in his life he was in love. The old song about it being a many-splendoured thing couldn't have been more wrong. This was torture—because if he told her how he felt and it turned out that she didn't love him, it would break his heart. And if he told her and she didn't believe him, it would be even worse.

Right now he was terrified of doing the wrong thing and pushing Becky even further away.

Although she'd told him a lot about her past, he was pretty sure she hadn't told him everything. That she was scared to trust, in case he hurt her. So the only thing he could do right now was the one thing that drove him completely crazy. Keep his promise—and wait. And hope that if he gave her enough space to miss him, then maybe she'd realise that what they had was special—that it was worth fighting for.

At least the hospital grapevine was quiet, Leandro thought during the week. Because they'd made it clear that when they were on duty they were strictly colleagues, nobody commented that they hadn't met for lunch for ages or snatched a coffee together at their break. And by some amazing luck nobody seemed to notice that they weren't together outside work or asked why.

Right now, what he needed was a distraction. Something to stop him thinking about Becky—stop missing her—every single second of the day.

Maybe, he thought, it was time he sorted out the other reason why he was in England. As distractions went, he couldn't get any bigger than this.

He'd had a few weeks now to get to know

Robert Cordell, the clinical director. On a professional basis, Leandro liked him. The older doctor was fair and clear-sighted. Leandro trusted his judgement. But that made Robert's actions of thirty-five years ago even more puzzling.

On a personal level, Leandro didn't know much more about him. Only that he wasn't married. And he could hardly start asking personal questions about Robert Cordell without people wondering why and talking. Gossip was the last thing he wanted right now.

He wished he could've talked to Becky about it. Maybe asked her advice about the best way to approach things. She might've been able to tell him a bit more about the clinical director, too.

But seeing as he'd promised her space and he needed her to know that he'd keep his word, it wasn't an option. So instead, at the end of his shift, he went up to see Robert Cordell.

'Leandro. Good to see you.' Robert smiled at him. 'I hear you've settled in very well.'

'I have, thank you.'

'So what can I do for you?'

Clearly the clinical director was expecting some request to do with work—extra staff or equipment for the emergency department, or maybe a suggestion about training.

'I…' How could he phrase this? And this really wasn't the right place for the kind of discussion he had in mind. 'I wondered if we could have a chat.'

'Of course. If it's about staying on when David's back, then I'd be very pleased. You're a real asset to this hospital,' Robert said.

Hmm. He might not think so when they'd talked. 'It isn't about work. It's…personal. Um, look, I know this probably isn't the done thing, but do you think we could have a quiet drink together somewhere?'

Robert frowned. 'Personal, you say.'

The wary expression on his face made Leandro suddenly realise what Robert was thinking: that Leandro was trying to make a move on him. It was enough to break the tension, and he laughed. 'Not *that* kind of personal.' He sobered. 'But…it's something that maybe neither of us would want overheard.'

'This sounds serious.'

'It is,' Leandro said quietly.

'Look, my secretary's gone for the day. Take

a seat. I'll make us both a coffee and close my office door.' Robert was as good as his word. A couple of minutes later he closed his office door behind him and brought two mugs of coffee over to this desk. 'So what's this all about?'

Leandro took a deep breath. 'There isn't a way around this so I'll ask you straight. Did you ever know a woman called Maricella García?'

Robert's expression suddenly went pinched. 'Yes. Why?'

'Her full name is Maricella García Herrera.' The clinical director looked at him, and Leandro saw the very moment the older man made the connection. 'You are her son?'

Leandro inclined his head in silence.

Robert exhaled sharply. 'I knew your mother when I was a student.'

'I know.'

'She told you about me?'

'Last year,' Leandro said.

'So your father—Señor Herrera—'

'There is no *el senyor* Herrera,' Leandro cut in quietly. 'I do not have my father's name. Only my mother's.' He felt a muscle in his jaw work. 'And she was very ill last year.'

'Maricella was ill?' Robert looked shaken. 'How is she now?'

Leandro was pleased to see the concern in Robert's eyes. 'She is fine, thank you. Or I would not have left Barcelona.'

'I haven't seen her for thirty-six y—' Robert stopped abruptly and pressed a hand to his chest. 'Oh, lord. And you're thirty-five, aren't you? So are you telling me you're my—?'

Not yet. Because he needed to know something first. 'Why did you leave Barcelona?' Leandro cut in.

Robert ignored the question. 'Are you my *son*?'

'Why did you leave Barcelona?' Leandro repeated.

Robert blew out a breath. 'Because my parents had a car accident. My dad was in hospital with a broken leg, and my aunt got a message to me in Barcelona to say I was needed at home to help look after my younger brother and sister.' Robert frowned. 'But I went to Maricella's house before I left Spain. I intended to tell her myself that I'd be back as soon as I could—that I'd write to her every day while I was back in England.'

'So why didn't you?'

'Because she wasn't there,' Robert said simply. 'The housekeeper said she was visiting an aunt with her mother. So I left her a note giving her my address in England and my phone number, telling her what had happened and that I'd be in touch as soon as I could.' His expression was grim. 'I wrote to her every single day for two months. I waited for the postman every morning, hoping for a reply. Day after day, there was nothing. And when it was time for me to go back to university in London and I still hadn't heard from her, I came to the realisation that maybe she wasn't that interested in me. That I'd been a holiday romance and it was over.'

Leandro knew how that felt. With Becky, he'd been as good as a holiday romance. OK, so they'd agreed up front that it wouldn't ever be permanent, but things had changed. He'd fallen in love with her.

'So you just got on with your life and forgot her?'

'Not quite. I got on with my life, yes. But I never forgot her. Nobody ever quite matched up to her.'

Yes, he knew that feeling, too. No other

woman had made him feel the way that Becky made him feel.

'So that's why you never married?'

'Do you have a dossier on me or something?'

'A sketchy one,' Leandro admitted wryly. 'But I couldn't exactly grill people about you without them asking me questions. Questions I didn't want to answer until I'd talked to you.'

'I would've done the same,' Robert admitted. 'So that's why you came to work here?'

'To find out for myself what you were like. *Sí*. So you never married?'

'No point, seeing as I wasn't going to marry the love of my life.' The words were simple, and Leandro could tell from Robert's expression that they were said with utmost sincerity. He'd loved Maricella. Deeply.

And Maricella had loved him back.

'My mother never forgot you either,' Leandro said softly.

'So she never married either?' Robert's blue eyes brightened with hope.

'No.'

A strange expression flickered on Robert's face. 'But she still had you. Even though her parents…'

'Weren't very happy about it,' Leandro said laconically.

'And you're my son.'

'Yes.'

Robert took a deep breath. 'I don't know what to say. I… Even in my wildest dreams, I never expected this.'

Exactly how he'd been when Becky had told him about the baby. Shocked. Too stunned to know how to react.

'If it makes you feel any better, it's strange for me, too. I imagined you as one of King Arthur's knights when I was a kid.' Leandro shrugged. 'Except obviously you never came to rescue my mother on your white charger.'

'If I'd known,' Robert said, his voice suddenly hard, 'things would have been different. If I'd had the slightest idea that Maricella was expecting my baby…I'd have gone back to Barcelona, kicked your grandparents' door down if they'd refused to admit me and carried her off back to England. And you'd have grown up with grandparents who would've spoiled you stupid, aunts and uncles who'd have doted on you, and a father who was there for you every minute of the day.'

Which was what Leandro wanted for his own child. Two parents who loved each other—and who were *together.*

Robert's expression grew grimmer. 'She didn't get a single one of my letters, did she? Or the note I left with the housekeeper. And I bet her parents had told anyone answering the door to lie to me and say that Maricella wasn't there.' He shook his head in a mixture of anger and disbelief. 'I shouldn't have been so trusting. Or so bloody proud. I should've gone back to Barcelona and camped on their doorstep until she saw me and told me herself that she didn't want to see me again.'

'You were, what, twenty?'

'Nineteen. I'd just finished the first year of my degree.'

'At that age,' Leandro said, 'and in those days, you accepted the word of your elders.' He shrugged. 'You weren't to know.'

'What I don't understand is why they didn't give her my letters once they knew she was expecting you.'

'They probably thought you'd deny everything. You weren't Catalan. And you were a student, right at the beginning of your career.'

Robert's eyes glittered with anger. 'What difference does that make? I would still have
married your mother and helped her bring you
up. It would've been hard, with me being a
student, but we'd have managed. Muddled
through together.' He gritted his teeth. 'I wish
I'd gone back. But I really thought she didn't
want to know. I thought she'd probably married
the son of some wealthy businessman.'

'The way her parents expected her to?'
Leandro smiled wryly. 'No. My mother did
things her way.'

'So I see.' Robert stared at him. 'Now I look
at you, I can see your mother in you. You have
her colouring.'

'She claims I have your nose.'

Robert took his wallet from the inside pocket of
his suit jacket, and fished out a photograph. 'Here.
It's the only one I have.' He handed it to Leandro.

'You've carried this photograph next to your
heart…?'

'Ever since I left Barcelona,' Robert said wryly.

Leandro touched the surface of the photograph. 'She was beautiful. Still is.' He handed
the photograph back, then fished out his own

wallet. Took out a much more recent photograph and handed it to Robert.

'You're right. She's still beautiful,' Robert said softly. His eyes were glittering suspiciously as he looked at Leandro. 'So where do we go from here?'

'Take it slowly, I guess, and get to know each other.' Leandro shrugged. 'I'm not doing anything special tonight. So if you're not either, maybe we could have dinner. Start to catch up on everything we've missed.'

'I'd like that,' Robert said. He handed the photograph back. 'I'd like that very much.'

As Leandro tucked the photograph back into his wallet, he caught a glimpse of the other photograph he carried. One from a photo booth, taken on impulse one afternoon as he and Becky had passed it. Both of them laughing, their faces pressed together.

His father had spent the past thirty-six years alone, missing the love of his life.

And Leandro hoped to hell that by giving Becky space now, he wasn't about to make the same mistake.

CHAPTER FOURTEEN

'GINNY SAUNDERS, aged thirty-six, abdominal pain,' Karen said, handing the notes to Becky.

Becky called out Ginny's name, and a white-faced woman lifted her hand. Becky went over to her. 'Would you like to come through with me?' she asked.

'Please…I can't take much more of the pain,' the patient whispered, her face white.

'We'll do our best to stop it,' Becky reassured her. 'If I can ask you a few questions before the doctor sees you, it'll help me narrow things down.' She turned to their receptionist. 'Karen, can you tell the next free doctor to come into cubicle three, please?' And, please, don't let it be Leandro, she added silently. He'd kept his word all week and given her space—and she hated the fact that she missed him so much. That she found herself looking for him at work.

Becky settled her patient on the bed. 'Do you want a glass of water before we start?'

'No, th— Ooh!' Ginny doubled up in pain.

Becky held her hand. 'How long has this been going on?' she asked gently.

'I was fine until three weeks ago. Then I couldn't stop throwing up and my stomach hurt so much. I came here for treatment.'

Becky quickly checked her notes. 'They gave you a proton pump inhibitor and the pain settled, so they discharged you.'

'And it's back again.'

'Is it the same sort of pain and the same place, Ms Saunders?'

She nodded. 'It's on my left side.'

'Does it move anywhere else?'

'No.'

Hmm. Probably not her appendix, but Becky wasn't ruling anything out yet. 'Are you feeling sick this time round?'

'No, but I'm losing weight because I can't face eating.'

'When you do eat, does anything in particular set off the pain?'

'No.'

'What about when you rest—does it help?'

Ginny shook her head.

'It says in your notes that you don't smoke and you drink maybe one or two glasses of wine a week. Is that still the case?'

'Yes.'

At that moment, the curtain twitched back.

The next free doctor.

And, of course, it had to be Leandro. He nodded acknowledgement to Becky and introduced himself to the patient. Becky brought him up to speed on Ginny's history, and Leandro took over the questioning.

'Does anything make the pain feel worse or better?'

'It's just there all the time.'

He glanced at Becky, and she knew he was thinking the same thing as she was: a potential ectopic pregnancy.

Please, don't let it be that, Becky begged silently. She wasn't sure she'd be able to handle that kind of emergency right now. Not when she'd only just discovered that she herself was pregnant.

'Are you taking any medication?' Leandro

asked. 'And I'm including anything recreational here.'

Ginny's eyes widened. 'Recreational?'

'It's not our place to report you or make life difficult for you,' he said softly, 'and I'm not going to give you any lectures, but I need to know so I can treat you safely.'

'I don't even smoke, let alone do drugs,' Ginny said wryly. 'I'm not on any tablets or anything, not even for hay fever, though I did have a contraceptive implant injection two months ago.'

Leandro nodded. 'Given that, I probably know what you're going to tell me next, but I need to ask anyway. Is there a possibility you might be pregnant?'

At the word 'pregnant', he looked at Becky. His expression was unreadable, and she quickly glanced away.

'I did a test three weeks ago, and it was negative,' Ginny said.

Negative.

Unlike Becky's.

And how Becky wished hers had stayed negative, so things could be back to how they had been between her and Leandro. And yet, at the same time…how could she wish his baby away? Guilt flooded through her. What sort of woman was she? Right now, she really didn't like herself.

'Would you let us do another test, just in case?' Leandro asked. At Ginny's nod, he said, 'I'd like to examine you now, then I'll give you some pain relief and I'll need you to do me a urine sample.'

Even before he'd said it, Becky was drawing up the analgesics she knew he was going to request, along with an antiemetic.

He gently examined Ginny's stomach. 'I can't feel anything out of the ordinary—no distension or any enlarged organs or any swelling.' He listened to her stomach through a stethoscope. 'I'm pleased to say that I can hear bowel sounds, so we don't have to panic just yet.' He straightened up, took the stethoscope off and smiled at her. 'Thank you for being patient with me, Ms Saunders. I'll give you something for the pain now.'

Becky handed him the syringe; Ginny shuddered and closed her eyes. 'Oh. That's better.'

'I'm going to give you an antiemetic as well,

because sometimes the pain relief can make you feel sick,' he said. 'And then could you do the urine sample for me while I have a quick word with my colleague?'

'Yes, of course.'

His colleague? Oh, lord. He meant *her*. And she had a nasty feeling that his 'quick word' meant personal stuff.

'My office,' he said to Becky, making her doubly sure that this was going to be about personal stuff.

Her hand was trembling slightly as she gave Ginny the empty sample bottle. 'If you can come back here afterwards, we'll join you,' she said gently. 'Try not to worry. Mr Herrera's very thorough—and he's very good.'

He was good at lots of other things, too, she thought as she walked over to Leandro's office. In fact, he'd be good at anything he tried to do. And the way he was with the children who came in to the ward…he'd be a fantastic dad.

Half of her knew she was being unreasonable about this. But the other half couldn't help the panic. The fear that everything was going to go wrong again. That her feelings for him wouldn't be enough to keep their relationship together.

She dragged in a breath when she saw his door was closed, and knocked once.

'Come in.'

She closed the door behind her, and remained leaning against the door. 'You wanted a quick word.'

He nodded. 'Just checking that you were all right.' At her frown of incomprehension, he added softly, 'Our patient needs a pregnancy test—and you and I both know there's the possibility of an ectopic pregnancy. I just thought you might find this a bit too close to home—too upsetting. Would you like me to get someone else to take the case?'

Becky had to swallow hard. Leandro was a good man. Kind. Thoughtful. So why couldn't she let herself trust him? Why couldn't she let the fear go?

'I'm fine,' she said, but her voice was wobbly. And from his expression she knew he'd noticed.

'If you change your mind a bit later on, it won't be a problem.'

'It's my job. And I don't back out of handling cases.'

'I wasn't suggesting for one minute that you

did.' He raked a hand through his hair. 'I'll put that remark down to hormones.'

'I'm sorry,' she whispered. 'You were being nice. I didn't mean to snap.'

'I know you didn't.' His eyes were soulful. 'I'm trying to give you time, Becky. But it's so hard.' He moistened his lower lip. 'I miss you. And I'm not talking about just sex. It's *you* I miss.'

She dragged in a breath. She missed him, too. Like crazy. The number of times she'd almost picked up the phone and called him…

All it would take would be one step.

One step and she could be in his arms.

Safe.

Except…taking that step meant taking a risk. Trusting him. And she couldn't get past the fact that marriage and children weren't on his agenda: he was focused on his career. She and the baby would take second place—or hold him back, meaning that he'd come to resent them and everything would go pear-shaped.

She couldn't do that.

She swallowed hard. 'We have a patient waiting for us.'

'Yeah.' He paused. 'You're absolutely sure you're OK?'

'I'm sure. Thank you,' she added.

'De res.'

The pregnancy test was negative.

Becky couldn't help exchanging a glance with Leandro, and she knew he was thinking exactly the same as she was. *Hers hadn't been.*

'Right. I need bloods—full blood count, platelets, liver function tests, bleeding and clotting times,' he said to Becky. 'And I want an ECG and ultrasound.' He turned to the patient. 'It's definite that you're not pregnant, Ms Saunders, so you'll be glad to know that rules out an ectopic pregnancy. But given the problems you had before, we're going to run some blood tests, and then I want to do an ultrasound of your abdomen—it's the same kind of scan a pregnant woman has, it's perfectly safe, and it's not going to hurt.' He smiled at her. 'It'll just give me a picture of what's going on inside. I might need to send you for a more detailed scan, depending on what the ultrasound shows, but nothing's going to hurt.'

At the word 'scan', Becky couldn't help

looking at him. She needed to book in with the midwife and have a dating scan. Would Leandro insist on going with her? Probably. But she needed to know it was because he wanted to, not because he felt it was his duty.

The ECG was perfectly normal. Becky sorted out the bloods—but when the ultrasound results were available Leandro frowned. 'I think we've found the culprit.'

Ginny went white. 'It's not cancer, is it? Please, tell me it's not cancer. I…I'm too young for this. I can't—'

'It's absolutely *not* cancer,' he cut in to reassure her, sitting on the edge of her bed and holding her hand. 'But there's a clot in one of your veins.'

'You mean, like DVT? But it can't be. I haven't been on a plane and my legs don't hurt.'

'It's a similar thing to DVT, just not in your legs. You have mesenteric venous thrombosis. What that means is that you have a blood clot blocking one of the major veins that drain blood from your intestine, so the blood supply to your bowel isn't as good as it could be. That's why you've got the pain.'

'What caused it?'

'It could be several things,' Leandro said, 'but my suspicion would be on the contraceptive injection. I'd recommend having the implant removed and using a different form of contraception in future.'

'Is the clot dangerous?' Ginny asked.

'It can cause some of the tissues to die, but if that's the case the surgeon should be able to fix it for you and you'll be fine.'

'Surgeon?' Her lower lip trembled. 'I have to have an operation?'

'The surgeon will be able to tell you that,' he said gently. 'I'm going to send you to Theatre for a laparoscopy—that's keyhole surgery, where they make a tiny cut in your abdomen and look inside so they can see if your bowel has been affected and whether you need surgery or whether it's something that will sort itself out once the clot has been removed. In the meantime, we can give you anticoagulant drugs to thin your blood and reduce the risk of another clot forming. Hopefully we've caught it early enough so you won't need an operation.'

'So that's what caused all the pain? One tiny little blood clot?'

'Yes.'

'So why did they miss it last time?'

'It's often misdiagnosed,' he said. 'Abdominal pain can be caused by so many different conditions. But because there didn't seem to be an obvious cause, I had a suspicion I wanted to check. You can only really tell mesenteric venous thrombosis if you're looking for it, through ultrasound and a CT scan—which, according to your notes, you didn't have last time.'

'Am I going to...?' Ginny swallowed hard, clearly unable to ask the question.

'Die? It's very unlikely.'

'And I've seen things on telly, where they have operations and end up with colostomy bags and all sort of...' She shuddered. 'I can't bear the idea of that. Who's going to want me if I've got a colostomy bag?'

'Again, that's unlikely to happen,' he said, still holding her hand. 'The surgeon will be able to tell you more. Because we've found the problem early enough, the chances are you might get away without an operation—or just a very small one where they resect a little part of your bowel. Try not to worry. I know it's hard and, of course, you're going to feel frightened, but our surgical team here is fantastic. I've watched them, and I can tell you I haven't seen better.'

Becky watched him as he calmed their patient down.

Leandro was the perfect doctor, kind and reassuring and knowledgeable.

The perfect *man*.

And here she was, pushing him out of her life, thinking about bringing up their child without him… He'd be a brilliant father, she thought again. How could she deprive her baby of a father who'd love him—or her—to bits?

But the alternative was to repeat her parents' mistakes. To repeat her own mistake of marrying a man who didn't want the same things she wanted—which would make him just as miserable and resentful as she would be. By opting out, she'd done the right thing for both of them.

So why did it feel so wrong? Why did it feel as if her heart was breaking?

CHAPTER FIFTEEN

BECKY was running scared. That much was obvious, Leandro mused. When he'd told her he missed her, he'd seen something in her expression. Just for a moment, before she'd dragged herself back into work mode. Something that had told him that she missed him, too.

But she was too scared to admit it. Scared that if she tried to make a go of it with him, it would end up like her first marriage maybe? Or scared that he'd only asked her to marry her because she was pregnant, and their relationship would end up like her parents'?

Well, he wasn't her father and he wasn't Michael.

And he'd been patient. She'd even admitted it herself.

So now was the time to start pushing. Just a little.

She was off duty now and although he wasn't

finishing until late, he was due a break. He glanced at his watch. Just enough time to get to the florist's.

He wrote the card himself. And paid enough to make sure it was delivered to Becky's house within the hour—or, if she was out, to the next-door neighbour.

And hopefully it would provoke a response.

Becky had never seen a bouquet this big—not even her wedding bouquet.

Fifty roses.

They weren't all red roses, which would've been over the top. No, these were crimson and blush-pink and baby pink and cream, toning beautifully. Feathery asparagus fern and deep green wrapping surrounded them.

They were absolutely beautiful.

And they made her want to bawl her eyes out.

But she managed to keep herself together and sign the delivery form before taking them inside. She didn't need to open the card to know who they were from—it was obviously Leandro—but she set the flowers on the kitchen table and opened the card.

I miss you. Something I need to talk to you about. Meet me for lunch tomorrow—the park opposite the hospital, at twelve-fifteen. Leandro xx

Something? What sort of something?

Terror gripped her for a moment. The baby? Some genetic problem?

No. Of course not. She really had to stop leaping to conclusions.

She texted him. *Thank you for the flowers. They're beautiful but you really didn't need to send them.*

A few seconds later, her phone beeped, signalling a text from Leandro. *I wanted to. Are you meeting me for lunch or not?*

She frowned, and texted back, *I thought you were off tomorrow.* And it was crazy that she should know his duty schedule as well as her own.

Beep. *I am.*

So why did he want to meet her for lunch? Quickly, she texted, *What did you want to talk to me about?*

This time her phone didn't beep to let her know it was a text message—it rang.

He knew she was around, so she couldn't get away with ignoring it. 'Hello?'

'Stop panicking,' he greeted her.

She crossed her fingers. 'I'm not.' But the fear was still there. 'Is it about the baby?'

'No. It's about my father.'

'You've talked to him?'

'Tell you tomorrow.'

Infuriating man. 'Why can't you tell me now?'

'Because.' He paused for just long enough to drive her crazy. 'See you at a quarter past twelve in the park. I'll be waiting.'

'Where?'

He laughed. 'The park isn't that big—you'll find me. See you tomorrow.'

Becky found it hard to concentrate at work, but finally it was five past twelve and she headed for the park opposite the hospital.

Leandro was sitting on a picnic blanket, leaning back against a tree, and there was a small hamper beside him.

'*Hola,*' he said quietly as she joined him. 'I noticed over the last few days that you tend to avoid the canteen, so I guessed you'd rather not have lunch anywhere near cooking smells.'

He'd noticed?

'So I thought a picnic in the open air might be more pleasant for you.' He smiled. 'It's not the picnic I would have made for you, but there are things you shouldn't be eating right now— *crema Catalan* being top of the list because of the raw eggs—and I thought food without scent would be easier for you.' He pulled a face. 'Which means this is the blandest, most boring picnic you'll ever eat.'

She really hadn't expected him to be that thoughtful. It made tears prick her eyelids. 'Thank you.'

He unpacked the hamper and set out the picnic. Among other things there were dry crackers, grapes, breadsticks, raw carrot and cucumber. 'Help yourself,' he said, pouring her a glass of water.

'I loved the flowers,' she said softly. 'Though you really didn't need to send them.'

'I wanted to.' He shrugged. 'So. No arguments, OK? I don't want to fight with you, Becky.'

'So why did you want to see me? You said it was about your father?'

He nodded. 'I'm going to tell you a story while you're eating.' He sat with his knees drawn up and his hands clasped loosely by his ankles. 'Once upon a time…' At her wry smile, he continued, 'Once upon a time, there was a young Catalonian woman. She was the only child of a lawyer with a large practice, and everyone expected her to marry the son of another lawyer with an equally large practice and the firms would merge. Except she fell in love with an English medical student who was travelling around Spain for the summer. He fell in love with her, too, and stayed in Barcelona instead of travelling around the country. Except then he left suddenly, without a word.

'He was the love of her life, and she was heart-broken. She didn't know how to get in touch with him. Although she asked around where he'd been staying, nobody had a forwarding address. He didn't call her, didn't write to her—he'd just vanished. Her parents did the whole "I told you so" routine and refused to talk about him.'

Leandro watched Becky's expression. It didn't

tell him a thing—and although she'd nibbled the corner of a cracker and sipped the glass of water he'd poured for her, she wasn't really eating.

So he continued talking. 'A few weeks later the girl realised she was expecting his baby. Although her family pressured her to get rid of the child or have it adopted, she refused. And she flatly refused to marry the other lawyer's son. Her parents more or less disowned her. But she and her son muddled through, and eventually her son followed in his father's footsteps and became a medic. She had several offers of dates, but she always turned them down. And years later she finally told him the truth about his father. And then the young—well, maybe not so young,' he corrected wryly, 'man decided to go to England and find his father. Except while he was there…' He spread his hands. 'Well, that's another story. One you already know. Anyway, he found his father. Talked to him. Discovered he liked the man. And then he found out the other half of the story.'

'What happened?'

'His parents were involved in a car crash and he was called home to help look after his younger brother and sister. He tried to get a message to his girlfriend in Barcelona but she never got it—and she also never got the letters he wrote to her every single day from England. So obviously she didn't write back. He waited for the postman every morning, and nothing arrived from Spain. He thought she'd changed her mind about him—that he was just a holiday romance and she was going to marry the lawyer's son. So finally he gave up. But nobody ever matched up to the love of his life, and he never married. He concentrated on his career instead and rose to the top of his profession.' He paused. 'He became clinical director of the hospital.'

Becky's eyes widened. 'You're telling me your father is Robert Cordell?'

Leandro inclined his head. 'And the son realised that his parents had never forgotten each other or fallen out of love with each other. So…' He shrugged.

'You can't leave the story there,' Becky protested.

'I don't know what happens next.' He spread his hands. 'With Robert's permission, I gave my mother his phone number. Maybe they'll talk, maybe they won't. But I hope they do. If nothing else, to lay the ghosts of the past to rest.' He paused. 'So. How are you?'

'I'm OK, thanks.'

She didn't look it. She was pale and there were dark shadows under her eyes. 'Aren't you going to ask me?' he prompted.

'How are you?'

'Miserable. Because I'm thinking that I take after my parents.'

She frowned. 'How?'

'Because it's taken me too long to work out what I really want from life.' At her silence, he added, 'You're supposed to ask me what that is.'

'I already know. You want to be clinical director and professor of medicine.'

'Wrong.'

'You told me so yourself.'

'Uh-huh. And I got it wrong. Because that's not what I want. I always said I didn't want a wife and children. But, actually, I do.'

Her face went paler still. 'That's what Michael wanted.'

'But I'm not Michael.' He kept his gaze fixed on hers. She had to listen to him. Hear what he was saying. Realise he meant it. 'I think I want a little more than Michael did. I want a wife who's her own person. A woman who's fulfilled—as my equal partner, *and* as the mother of my children, *and* in whatever role she chooses. If my wife decides she doesn't want a career break after our baby arrives, that's fine— we'll work something out between us.' He took her hand. 'I'm not your father, Becky. I don't want to marry you because of the baby. Well, I do,' he amended, 'because I want to see our children grow up. I want to read bedtime stories and do bathtime and be there when they wake with a bad dream. I don't want to be a weekend father, someone whose love is measured in trips to the park and ice creams. I don't want to be a school-holidays father with my child growing up in England and coming to Barcelona for visits at half-term or what have you. I want to be there, so our children grow up knowing that both parents love them.'

She lifted her chin. 'Getting married for the sake of the children really isn't the right reason to get married.'

'It's only part of the reason,' he cut in. 'I want you for your own sake.'

'Supposing we do get married.' She swallowed hard. 'When you realise I'm not The One it'll all go wrong and it'll be even messier once children are involved.'

'I'm not Michael,' he reminded her again. 'I don't want you to fit into any preconceived ideas of what my wife should be. I want you to be yourself. My other half. The woman who makes me complete. And I think you're The One, Becky, because I've never felt about anyone the way I feel about you. That scared me stupid, and it was a long time before I could admit it to myself.'

'There's something I haven't told you.' She closed her eyes. 'After Michael left me—when his lover was pregnant—I found out that I was pregnant, too.'

He said nothing, just reached out and wrapped his fingers round hers. Squeezed her fingers very briefly, letting her know he was there for her.

'I didn't tell him. I didn't tell anyone. And then I…' She swallowed hard. 'I lost the baby,' she whispered. 'At about twelve weeks. And I felt so *guilty*.'

'It wasn't your fault, *estimada*. You know as

well as I do that many women lose a baby in the first twelve weeks. These things happen.'

'It was my fault,' she repeated. 'Because I didn't want the baby enough. And when I lost the baby, I was…' She lifted her chin. 'I really don't like myself for this, but I was relieved. I was upset at the same time—of course I was upset—but my overwhelming feeling was relief that I wasn't going to be trapped, wasn't going to have to stay married to Michael.' She bit her lip. 'What kind of woman am I, not wanting to have that baby?'

'A very human one.' He rubbed the pad of his thumb over the backs of her fingers. 'Michael had cheated on you, he'd hurt you, he hadn't supported your career and he'd expected you to be the one making all the sacrifices. Every time you looked at the baby you'd see him, and you'd see a child who hadn't been conceived out of love.'

She rubbed at her eyes, refusing to shed tears—though he guessed that she'd cried her heart out several times over this. And he also guessed what she wasn't telling him—that she was afraid she wouldn't love their baby.

Given her difficult childhood, she was probably scared she was going to turn into her mother.

'But I know the kind of woman you are,' he said gently. 'I've seen you with the kids on the ward—you're comforting and calming and kind. And that's with children you don't know—with your own children, there'll be an extra bond. I'm sure if you hadn't miscarried, you'd have made a brilliant mother to your child. And you're going to be a brilliant mother to our baby.'

She was silent.

'Becky? Talk to me,' he said softly.

She dragged in a breath. 'Supposing I'm like my mother? Supposing I don't love the baby?'

The fact she'd trusted him with her deepest fears, ones that maybe she hadn't dared admit to herself before, gave him hope. 'You're *not* your mother. For a start, you wouldn't be worrying about loving the baby if you were your mother. If you were selfish and unable to love, it wouldn't even occur to you,' he pointed out. 'And you can stop worrying about bonding, too. Not every woman falls in love with her baby straight away. Sometimes it takes a while. But it will come.'

'But how do you *know*?'

'Because,' he said quietly, 'I grew up knowing I was loved. Every single day. I'm sorry you had a horrible childhood. But I'm also sure that, because of it, you'll try your hardest to make sure it's not like that for your own child.'

Becky closed her eyes. 'I'm scared. If I marry you…how do I know it's not going to go wrong, the way it did with Michael? I loved him and he loved me. And it ended in a mess.'

'I'm not Michael,' he said. How many times was he going to have to say it before she believed him? 'Look, I know Spanish men have a reputation for being domineering. I could bulldoze you into a wedding, sweep you along and tell you everything would be all right.'

She opened her eyes and gave him a wry smile. 'But you're not Spanish, you're Catalonian.'

'*Sí*, and there's another reason why I'm not going to push you into this. I can make the doubts go away for a while—but they'll come back again. Until you're sure of me, sure of yourself, marrying isn't the right thing to do.' He lifted her hand to his mouth and kissed the back of her hand. 'So, much as it pains me to do this,

I'll wait until you're ready. Until you believe in me. Because I love you, and you mean too much for me to risk losing you by pushing you.'

He'd said he loved her.

She believed him.

But she still couldn't make the fears and the doubts go away.

After lunch, Leandro insisted on walking Becky back to the hospital. She was silent all the way there, not knowing what to say.

He loved her.

For herself.

And she knew she'd fallen for him, too. But if she told him…would it make everything go wrong, the way it had with Michael?

Part of her thought she was just being hormonal. Seeing problems where there weren't any.

But part of her still wasn't ready to take the risk.

'I'll see you on shift tomorrow, then,' he said.

'Day off.'

'You changed your shifts so you wouldn't have to work with me?' he guessed.

She felt her face heat. 'Um…'

He sighed. 'Ah, Becky. All right. I'll tell you

how it's going to be. Every day I'm going to tell you I love you. And one day you'll be ready to hear that. One day you'll be ready to say it back to me.'

Right now she couldn't say the words to him. But there was one thing she could do. 'I have an appointment on Tuesday at ten. If you, um, want to be there.'

His eyes widened. 'An antenatal appointment?'

'A dating scan.'

'Of course I want to be there. You're not doing this alone. We made this baby together.' He gave her that slow, sexy smile that always made her knees go weak. 'And we're going to look after it together, too.'

Fear skittered through her again. If she let herself believe… What if things changed, the way they had with Michael?

It must have shown in her expression, because he sighed. 'Relax. I'm not going to push you. I'll see you…whenever. And I'll definitely be there at the scan. I promise.'

'OK.' She started to walk through the hospital door.

'And, Becky?'

She turned on her heel to face him. 'Yes?'

'There's something I need to tell you.' He paused. *'T'estimo.* I love you.'

Just as he'd promised, he told her every day.

The next day, it was via a text message.

The day after—when she was still off duty—he had a single red rose delivered. He'd written the card himself. *In the language of flowers: I love you.*

The following day—when she was on an early shift—he sent her an email. *Look in your top left-hand drawer.*

She did. On top of a notebook, there was a sticky note. *LH ♥ RM.*

And the day after that there was a box on her desk, tied with a ribbon. Inside was a chocolate heart, inscribed very carefully with the words 'I love you'.

She called him that night. 'You're relentless.'

'I think the word you're looking for is steadfast. Or dependable. Or possibly even stubborn. But I did warn you that I'd tell you every day. I love you, Becky. And I'm pretty sure you love me, too. You just need to trust me—and trust yourself.' He paused. 'How are you feeling?'

'Still sick,' she admitted.

'I take it you've tried sniffing lemons and drinking ginger tea.'

'The lemons don't work and I can't bear the tea.'

'Uh-huh. Then I'll see you on the ward tomorrow. Oh, and, Becky?'

'Yes?'

'I love you.'

And then he put the phone down. Just before she said softly, 'I love you, too.'

When she went to her office the next day there was another box on her desk, tied with ribbon.

These are meant to be good. Try them.

She opened the box. Acupressure bands—used for travel sickness. And there was a sticky note wrapped round one of them. *P.S. I love you.*

He was crazy. Had to be. Because she was prickly and hormonal and miserable and impossible to please right now. But he was being so patient with her.

Maybe she'd feel differently after the scan. Once they'd seen their baby—together. Maybe then the fear would go away and it would be all right.

CHAPTER SIXTEEN

ON TUESDAY morning at twenty minutes to ten, Leandro was doing paperwork in his office. He wasn't officially due in the department until lunchtime, but he hadn't been able to settle at home. And although he'd been tempted to ring Becky and ask her if he could take her in to the clinic, he had a nasty feeling she'd see it as pushing her. He'd promised her space. And support. So this was the best option: keep himself occupied until about ten minutes before the appointment and then walk very slowly down to the ultrasound department. And try not to seem too much like an eager puppy when she walked through the door.

'Leandro? Oh, thank goodness you're here!' Mina came bursting into his office. 'I know you're not officially on duty but I can't find Martin—' the registrar on duty for that shift

'—and he's not answering his pager, and Ed's called from the ambulance on the way in with an emergency, a patient with chest pain and vomiting. ETA about thirty seconds ago.'

Thanks to a mixture of holidays and sickness, they were understaffed at the moment. No wonder she was worrying.

'Calm down, Mina,' he said gently. 'Everything's going to be fine. Deep breaths and count to five.'

'Yes, Leandro. Sorry for panicking.' She flushed.

'Don't worry about it. This is your first job, and I'm still just about young enough to remember how it felt.' He smiled at her. 'Feeling a bit of adrenaline is good news for your patients—it means you realise you don't know absolutely everything—but take things steady and it all slots into place a lot easier. Get someone to page Martin again and tell them to keep trying, and I'll stay until he gets here, OK?'

'OK. Thanks.'

He glanced at the clock. Nineteen minutes until he had to be in the scan. Three minutes to get to Ultrasound, if he ran from the emergency department. At least they were on the same floor, which helped. And clinics often overran. With luck, he'd still be able to make it, even if Martin cut it fine and took twenty minutes to get back to the department from wherever he was.

No way could he refuse to treat an emergency patient who desperately needed his help. And no way was he going to leave their foundation doctor to cope with a situation where she was out of her depth.

So he'd just better hope that Martin answered his pager.

Soon.

'Geoff Hadley, aged sixty,' Ed said as he wheeled the trolley into Resus. 'He had a bit of pain in his left chest and abdomen last night, so he thought if he had an early night he might feel better. But this morning he woke up and vomited, the pain got worse and radiated to his shoulder, so he called us. He's never had anything like this before, doesn't smoke, and drinks maybe two pints on Fridays in the pub with his friends. I've given him analgesia and an antiemetic, and we've called his daughter, who's on her way. Oh, and we did an ECG on the way in.' He handed Leandro the trace.

'Thanks, Ed,' Leandro said. 'Mr Hadley, I'm Leandro Herrera, the consultant. Would you mind if I examine you?'

'That's fine.' The older man looked worried. 'Am I having a heart attack?'

'The ECG—that's just a picture of what your heart's doing—says your heart rhythm's normal but a bit fast. So it's unlikely to be a heart attack.'

'But the pain and being sick… One of my friends died from bowel cancer. Is it that?'

'Try not to worry,' Leandro said gently. 'I'll know a bit more as soon as we've run some tests. Irene,' he said to the staff nurse, 'can you check Mr Hadley's blood pressure, temperature, pulse and respirations, please?'

Again he glanced at the clock. Come on, Martin. Answer the damned pager, he urged silently. Becky would be in the ultrasound department soon. He'd promised to be there. And he didn't want to let her down—not with something as important as this. It'd shatter her trust in him completely.

Mr Hadley was pale and sweaty; his skin felt clammy to the touch.

'Pyrexic,' Irene reported when she checked his temperature. 'Pulse regular, a hundred and six.'

Too fast, Leandro thought.

'Respirations forty a minute. Blood pressure's ninety-two over fifty-two.'

Not good. Like his pulse, his breathing was too fast, and his blood pressure was too low. 'I'm just going to listen to your chest, Mr Hadley,' Leandro said gently. 'Irene, can you sort the notes, please?' He glanced surreptitiously at his watch as he took his stethoscope from where he'd slung it round his neck. The minutes weren't just ticking by, they were galloping by. Where the hell was Martin? Leandro needed to be in Ultrasound with Becky right now.

But how could he just walk out and leave his patient?

Caught between a rock and a hard place. Whatever he did, he'd help one and hurt the other.

Why hadn't the registrar answered his bleep?

'Jugular venous pulse and heart sounds normal, Irene,' Leandro said, and the staff nurse dutifully wrote it down. 'Mr Hadley, I'm just going to tap your chest very lightly—I'll try not to hurt you, but just tell me if you're uncomfortable.'

'All right,' the older man croaked.

'Left lung base dull on percussion, air entry diminished.' He removed his stethoscope. 'I'm going to examine your abdomen now, Mr Hadley. Again, I'll try not to hurt, but tell me if it's sore.'

'Ouch, here. And here.'

'I'm sorry. And you're doing very well. Irene, can you note down soft abdomen with general tenderness? I'm going to just listen to your abdomen now, Mr Hadley. Mmm, normal bowel sounds.'

'So what's wrong with me?' the patient asked.

'I need to do some more tests before I can narrow it down. I'm going to need a blood sample and blood gases—which I'm afraid does hurt a tiny bit more than normal blood tests—and I'm going to send you for an X-ray and what we call a CT scan of your chest and abdomen so we can see what's going on inside you. I'm going to keep you nil by mouth for the time being, but I will ask you to swallow a contrast medium before your scan to help show me what's going on.'

* * *

Becky scanned the waiting room as she walked in. There were plenty of men sitting there—but not the one she wanted to see.

She glanced at her watch. Ten to. Well, she was early. Maybe he'd turn up in a minute. Knowing Leandro, he'd probably have to run down from the ward. But all the same it niggled her. She'd given him reasonable notice of today. OK, so she hadn't expected him to actually take a day off and go with her. He'd said he'd meet her here, which she'd interpreted as meaning he'd use his break time. But he could've changed his off duty from an early to a late to make absolutely sure he wasn't in the middle of an emergency.

She flicked through a pregnancy magazine, not really taking in any of the articles. And every time she glanced at her watch she was dismayed to find that only a few seconds had passed.

But the seconds added up and she grew twitchier and twitchier as the minutes passed.

Where on earth was he?

Had it slipped his mind what today was?

She was almost tempted to ring the emergency department to remind him that she was here.

Then again, if this was important enough to him, he'd remember. He'd be here.

She just had to be patient.

Swiftly Leandro sorted the blood tests and gases with Irene's help, and she accompanied Mr Hadley to his X-ray and scan. Before Leandro introduced himself to Mr Hadley's daughter, he took Mina to one side. 'Where the *hell* is Martin?' he asked, his voice low and urgent.

'I don't know. I've tried paging him.'

'Then page him again. For pity's sake, I'm not even meant to be on duty until this afternoon!'

She stared at him, looking utterly shocked.

Leandro sighed. 'Sorry, Mina. This isn't your fault. I shouldn't take it out on you.' He couldn't even tell her why he was so wound up or where he was going and why it was so important to him. It wasn't his place to announce Becky's pregnancy—she'd tell people about the baby when she was ready.

But if he didn't get to the ultrasound department soon, everything would go pear-shaped.

Oh, hell. He couldn't even ring Ultrasound and leave her a message. It'd be on the hospital grapevine in a flash—despite patient confidentiality, someone would overhear and put two and two together and make ten.

This was an impossible situation. He couldn't let Becky down—she needed him. But he couldn't let the department down either.

Where the hell was Martin?

A young woman waiting outside Resus looked close to tears. Leandro had already been told she was Mr Hadley's daughter. He needed to explain to her what was happening with her father and see if he could get any extra information about his health.

Ten o'clock. Right on cue, the midwife called, 'Becky Marston?'

Becky got to her feet and took a last look round the waiting room.

There was no sign of Leandro.

Which confirmed her worst fears. He was putting his career before her and the baby. Becky had always known that would be the case, whatever his protests that he wasn't like Michael.

Looks as if we're in this on our own, kid, she

thought, placing a protective hand across her still-flat abdomen, because he's not going to turn up.

By the time Irene brought Mr Hadley back from his X-ray and scans, the blood test results were back.

But Martin wasn't.

And Leandro was near screaming pitch.

If he didn't go now he was going to miss the scan.

Miss seeing his baby on the screen.

Miss sharing such an important moment with Becky, a moment that he'd been so looking forward to.

This couldn't be happening.

Please, let them be running late. Please, let him make it before she left.

It took a real effort to go through the tests and make sure he concentrated on them properly, for his patient's sake. 'Blood count, liver-function test, serum electrolytes and serum amylase normal,' Leandro said. 'Mild metabolic acidosis.' He flicked into the computer to check the X-rays. It looked very much like a hydropneumothorax to him. There was no free gas under the diaphragm, but the CT scan pictures confirmed his suspicion that there was air outside the oesophagus. His patient had Boerhaave's syndrome—vomiting increased the pressure against the wall of the oesophagus and tore it. Luckily it looked as if they'd caught the problem in the early stages, so it could be fixed through surgery.

Once he'd spoken to the surgeon and arranged the slot in Theatre, he explained to Mr Hadley and his daughter what was happening.

'When you were sick, Mr Hadley, you ruptured your oesophagus—that's the tube that carries food from your mouth to your stomach. So I'm going to send you to the surgical team in Theatre—they'll repair the damage.'

'So is he going to be able to eat again?' Mr Hadley's daughter asked.

'When the wound has healed, yes. But in the meantime we're going to need to keep him in hospital because we need to do what we call a jejunostomy—that's a small opening onto his skin from his bowel, and we'll feed you by tube, Mr Hadley, to make sure you get all the nutrients you need. You'll also have a chest drain in for a while after the operation to take away any fluids that shouldn't be there. But when you leave us, everything should be fine.' He forced himself to smile at them. 'The surgeon will be down shortly to introduce himself to you, and he'll be able to answer any questions. If there's anything else you're worried about or not sure about, get one of the team to call me and I'll come and talk to you.'

'Thank you, Doctor,' Mr Hadley's daughter said. 'When I got the call, I thought Dad...' Her voice faded and she bit her lip hard.

Leandro patted her hand. 'I know. It's always worrying when you get a call, even if you're a doctor. My mum was in hospital last year, so I know exactly how you feel.'

He took a surreptitious glance at his watch.

Oh, no. Oh, no, no, no.

Not only was he not going to make it for her appointment, he was in serious likelihood of missing her completely. And because he hadn't turned up, no way would she wait around for him.

He had to go.

Everyone would think he was being rude—

well, that was tough. The important thing was that his patient was stable. He'd smooth anything else over later. 'Look, I'm really sorry about this, but I need to be somewhere. As I said, if there's anything worrying you, get one of the team to call me. But I really have to go now.'

Completely ignoring the look of surprise on his colleagues' faces, he rushed out of the department.

Please, please, please, let there be a queue in Ultrasound. Let there be some kind of hold-up. Some kind of admin mix-up that meant nobody was hurt or in an emergency but Becky's scan would be delayed.

Please.

He pulled the door open and scanned the room swiftly. No Becky. Was she still in the ultrasound room?

Then he glanced at the doors at the other end of the department—and saw her about to walk through them. Not caring who stared at him, he bellowed, 'Becky!'

She turned and looked at him.

And the expression on her face chilled him.

This had all gone hideously, hideously wrong.

At least she waited until he'd crossed the department to join her, and let him walk outside with her so they'd have a tiny measure of privacy.

'I'm so sorry,' he said.

But before he could explain she lifted one hand. 'Save your breath, Leandro,' she said quietly. 'You weren't there. And that tells me more than any words can.'

'Becky—'

'No. I'm sorry. I can't do this. It's over,' she cut in.

And then she simply turned and walked away.

Becky spent a sleepless night, sick to the soul because Leandro had let her down, and being sick because her body clearly hadn't heard of morning sickness and believed in morning, afternoon, evening and night sickness.

Nausea might mean that her hormone levels were good, but it was small comfort when she was retching into the toilet every couple of hours.

The following morning her eyes felt gritty and swollen and she had a headache, but she dragged herself into work.

Leandro was off duty. Just as well, because

she really didn't feel up to facing him. It wasn't until her break, when she was sipping water in the staffroom, that Mina spoke quietly to her.

'Leandro was acting really strangely yesterday.'

Becky wriggled in her seat and tried to act nonchalant. 'Oh?'

'I've never, ever known him keep looking at his watch before—and he kept nagging me to keep trying Martin's pager.' Mina shook her head. 'Weird. He never usually minds helping out when he's not officially on duty.'

Becky went cold. 'What do you mean, not officially on duty? I thought he was on an early yesterday?'

'He changed it to a late—he said there was something he had to do yesterday morning, but he wouldn't say what it was. Just that it was important. He'd only come in to catch up on some paperwork. I don't know if it was a job interview or something…' Mina clapped her hand to her mouth. 'Oh, no. If it was, I stuffed it up big time for him.'

'How?'

'We had an emergency in and Martin wasn't answering his pager so I had to ask him for help—it turned out to be a case of Boerhaave's syndrome. I haven't seen one before.'

'They're not that common,' Becky agreed. 'So did Leandro do whatever it was he had to do yesterday?' she asked, as casually as she could.

'Well, he disappeared the first second he could—but I don't think he made his interview because he was in a vile temper for the rest of the day.' Mina grimaced. 'The patients would never have known it because he was as professional and sweet as he always is, but he barely said a word to anyone else in the department.'

Oh, lord.

How she'd misjudged him.

She hadn't even let him explain yesterday, she'd been so hurt and angry with him.

And he really had tried to put her first. He'd changed his shift to make sure he was there for her. Except he'd been caught up in an emergency. Of course he couldn't have walked out on an unstable patient, not if there was nobody to cover him.

'I doubt it was a job interview,' Becky said gently, knowing perfectly well where Leandro had planned to be. And he hadn't told anyone what it was: he'd kept her secret. He'd waited for her to be ready to tell people.

And she'd been completely unfair to him.

She needed to fix this. Right now.

Excusing herself, she grabbed her bag from her locker and went into the corridor to use her mobile phone. She called Leandro's home number and waited. The phone rang three times and clicked through to the answering-machine.

This was a message she definitely didn't want to leave to a machine.

She tried his mobile, but it was switched off.

All right. She'd go to his place after work. And she'd sit on his doorstep until he came home, if need be. Because she really, really needed to talk to him.

Becky went straight to Leandro's house after her shift. To her relief, he answered the door when she rang. But he looked absolutely terrible, as if he'd slept as badly as she had the previous night. He hadn't shaved, his hair was sticking up all over the place, and there were lines of strain on his face.

'Why didn't you tell me what happened yesterday?' she asked.

'You didn't exactly give me the chance,' he said dryly.

'I'm sorry. I've been such a cow.'

'Hormones,' he said dryly.

She shook her head. 'Lots of things. Can I come in?'

For a moment she thought he was going to refuse. Then he sighed and stood aside, letting her in. He ushered her into his living room and she sat on the sofa. 'About yesterday. I was so angry with you, so hurt. When you didn't turn up, I thought you'd put your work first. Before me and the baby.'

He slumped down opposite her in a chair. 'I'm not perfect, Becky. I'm not a hero. Just a man. And I'm going to let you down sometimes, just as you'll let me down sometimes.' He sighed. 'OK, so it was stupid of me to go into work before the scan, but I couldn't settle to anything at home and I thought I'd be better off at my desk, keeping busy.'

'And then an emergency came in,' she said softly.

'I'm an emergency doctor. I can't refuse to treat someone. It's what I do—it's who I *am*.'

She nodded. 'I know that.'

'I couldn't live with myself if I left a patient in need of treatment. I honestly intended to hand over to Martin halfway through, but it turned out he'd gone home with a migraine.' Leandro looked grim. 'The message hadn't got through to anyone so we didn't manage to replace him, and he'd switched his pager off—so nobody could track him down. All we knew was that he wasn't answering his bleep, we were short-staffed, and Mina was in a panic.'

'You couldn't leave her to cope in Resus on her own,' Becky agreed. 'She hasn't had enough experience.'

'I swear, I tried my hardest not to let you down. I meant to be there.'

'Mina said you were clockwatching.'

'I had every intention of being there at the scan, Becky. And I'm so sorry I missed it. I really wanted to see our baby. With you.'

She knew that now. He'd even changed his off-duty.

He dragged in a breath. 'So is everything OK with you and the baby?'

She nodded. 'I'm ten weeks, the baby looks fine, and the placenta's in the right place.'

'Good.' He swallowed hard. 'Becky, I don't know what to say any more. I've told you how I feel about you. That I love you. That I'm not like your father, intending to marry you out of a sense of duty because you're pregnant. I want to marry you for *you*, because I want to wake up with you in my arms every morning and know that whatever happens to me that day, life is still good because you're in it.' He closed his eyes briefly. 'I know I said I didn't want children, but I've worked through that now. I've realised that it wasn't because I didn't want a family at all—it was because I hadn't met the person I wanted to be a family with. Until you.'

The lump in Becky's throat was so huge, she couldn't say a word.

'And I know I wasn't supportive enough when you told me you were pregnant. I'm sorry. I was just…shocked, I guess. So I understood exactly how Robert felt when he found out I was his son—shocked and not knowing what to say because he'd never really thought about having children before.' He dragged in a breath. 'I should've told you I was delighted—that I would like nothing more than to have children with you, a family to share my love. And it's true, Becky. I'm so, so sorry that I screwed it up.'

She still hadn't said anything. And there were tears running down her face.

Leandro couldn't stand being apart from her any longer. And he didn't have anything left to lose any more. So he went over to the sofa, scooped her up and settled her on his lap, holding her close. 'Don't cry,' he whispered, stroking her hair. 'I know I let you down, but give me a chance to make it up to you.'

'It's not your fault,' she whispered. 'It's mine. Because I've been too scared to take risks. Too scared to trust you. Too ready to push you away to make sure I didn't get hurt—except being apart from you hurts.' She wrapped her arms round him, hugging him. 'I…I'm sorry, Leandro. I know you're a good man and I should trust you.'

'But after Michael and your father, it's hard.'

'I'm sorry,' she whispered again.

He knew he was pushing, but he couldn't help the question. 'So where does that leave us?'

'I love you.' She shuddered. 'Though it terrifies the hell out of me.'

His arms tightened round her. 'Hey. We can work on the trust thing. Together. As long as I know you love me, too, it'll work itself out. We'll fight a bit. And then we get the fun of making up.' He brushed his mouth against hers. 'A small lesson in Catalan. Repeat after me. *T'estimo*. I love you.'

'*T'estimo*,' she repeated.

'*T'estimo molt.*'

'What's *molt*?'

'Very much,' he translated. 'And I do. I love you more than I ever thought possible.' He paused, looking her straight in the eye. 'Becky, even if you don't want to get married—and I understand it'd be hard for you, after what happened with Michael—I want you to move in with me.'

'Here?'

'If you like the house, maybe we can persuade the owner to sell it to us. If not, we'll choose somewhere else. Together. A place for our family.'

'But… We can't buy a house.' She frowned. 'You're only here on secondment. Six months, you said.'

'I want more than six months,' he said softly. 'I can extend my secondment. Or get a permanent job over here. Or we could go to Barcelona and work over there. It doesn't matter where we are, as long as we're together.' He stroked her face. 'And I want to make it very clear that I don't expect you to sit at home and look after the baby. Not unless you want to. We'll work something out between us.'

'What about you wanting to be clinical director? I'd be holding you back.'

'No, you wouldn't. There's all the time in the world. I'm only thirty-five. I'll get there— just a bit more slowly than I originally planned.' He smiled. 'Which is a good thing, actually, because my life's got a different perspective now. A better one. There's more to it than just my career.' He stole another kiss. 'I understand what my mother meant now about not settling for second best. I know that concentrating on my career would be settling for second best—because it'd mean I don't have you and our baby. And that's not what I want.' He stroked her face. 'I want you. With me. *Sempre*. For always.'

'I want that, too.' She brushed the hair back from his forehead. 'I love you, Leandro. *T'estimo molt.*'

He could practically hear the 'but', even though she didn't say it. And he didn't want there to be any more secrets, any more mis-understandings. 'But?' he asked softly.

She took a deep breath. 'What if I…what if I lose the baby?'

He could understand her fear. She'd lost Michael's baby at twelve weeks. And right now she was ten weeks pregnant with their baby. The next fortnight was going to be gruelling for her—every time she went to the loo she'd be checking for blood. Worrying. 'There's no reason why you should lose this baby. Having one miscar-riage doesn't necessarily mean you'll have a second,' he said, holding her tightly. 'But if the unthinkable does happen, you won't be alone. I'll be with you every step of the way. And then we take it slowly. Together. *Passi el que passi*—whatever comes. If we're blessed with children, then I'm happy. If we're not, I'm still happy, because I'll be with you and I love you. And everything's going to work out just fine.'

She was silent for what felt like for ever. And then she smiled. 'I believe you,' she said softly.

EPILOGUE

Seven months later

LEANDRO sat on the hospital bed, as close as he could get to Becky, with their newborn daughter on his lap.

'I can't believe we're so lucky. How perfect she is. And we made her.' He stroked one finger against the baby's soft cheek. 'Estrella. It's the perfect name for her. Because she's a star.'

Becky laughed. 'Only a couple of hours old, and she can wrap you round her little finger.'

'Excuse me,' Leandro retorted. 'And who admitted she'd fallen in love the very first second she held her daughter?'

'Yeah.' She leaned forward and stole a kiss. 'I was so scared it wouldn't happen. That I wouldn't know how to bond.'

'We've been practising for six months,' he

reminded her with a grin. 'Not that I intend to stop practising.'

He'd told her every single day that he loved her. Just as she told him. And at last all the fears had gone away.

More than that—he'd put her relationship with her parents on a different footing. He'd charmed them and put them very straight about his views on Becky's job. For the first time they actually seemed to value what she did, who she was.

And it didn't matter that they weren't married. She was more secure than she'd ever been in her life.

She shifted slightly, drawing closer to him. 'You know, I was thinking. Estrella would look so gorgeous as a flower girl.'

'Flower girl? As in a bridesmaid? You've been planning a wedding?'

She shrugged. 'I had to think of something to get me through the first few hours of labour pains. While I was waiting for you to come home.'

He gave her a pointed look. 'I told you, the second your contractions started, I'd be there. If you'd called me…'

'There was no point until the contractions

were getting closer together. And of course I knew you'd come home as soon as I called.' She stole a kiss. 'Chill out, *estimat.* I've come a long way in the last six months.'

'I know.'

'So, as I was saying, Estrella as flower girl.'

He caught his breath. 'Are you suggesting the m-word for *us*?'

She smiled. 'I believe it's traditional for the man to suggest it. And I mean suggest—not just tell me, like you did last time.'

'When you said no.'

'Try me now.'

He gave her a broad smile. 'You'll have to take the down on one knee bit as read. Rebecca Marston, I love you and our daughter more than I ever thought possible. Will you marry me?'

She smiled. 'Yes.'

He was kissing her deeply when there was a knock at the door.

'*Hola,*' he called.

'Just wanted to pop in and see my brand-new granddaughter.' Robert stood in the doorway. 'If you don't mind.'

'Of course we don't,' Becky said immediately.

'If you hadn't come down, Leandro would've come up to your office to fetch you.' She and Leandro hadn't been the only ones who'd become new parents and needed to adjust. And over the last six months Leandro and his father had become closer.

'There's someone else who's dying for a cuddle with the baby,' Robert said, ushering Maricella into the room before them.

'Mama?' Leandro's eyes widened and then he beamed at her. 'I thought you wouldn't be here until tomorrow. You were supposed to ring me and let me know when your flight got in so I could meet you.'

'You think I could wait that long to see my granddaughter?' Maricella teased.

Becky prodded him. 'Hand her over. It's a bit difficult to get him to put her down,' she explained to Maricella.

'Oh-h-h,' Maricella breathed as she sat down and Leandro gently transferred the baby to her arms. 'She's beautiful. Like you were as a baby.'

Robert sat on the arm of the chair. 'Mari, I wish…'

She looked up at him, 'Me, too,' she said

softly. 'But we've been given a second chance with the next generation.' She smiled at Leandro and Becky. 'She's gorgeous. I was right to book the first flight I could. And Robert picked me up from the airport.'

Becky and Leandro exchanged a glance.

'Are you telling me…?' Leandro asked.

Robert and Maricella smiled at each other, and then at him. 'You gave your mother my number. It took her a while, but she called me. And we've been talking ever since,' Robert explained.

'And Robert came out to Barcelona to see me last month,' Maricella added.

Leandro just stared.

'As your mother says, we've been given a second chance,' Robert said, 'and we're going to make the most of it.'

'Amen to that,' Becky said softly. Leandro was her second chance at happiness, and she knew for certain this time it was going to work.

MEDICAL™

Large Print

Titles for the next six months…

March

SHEIKH SURGEON CLAIMS HIS BRIDE Josie Metcalfe
A PROPOSAL WORTH WAITING FOR   Lilian Darcy
A DOCTOR, A NURSE: A LITTLE MIRACLE Carol Marinelli
TOP-NOTCH SURGEON, PREGNANT NURSE Amy Andrews
A MOTHER FOR HIS SON   Gill Sanderson
THE PLAYBOY DOCTOR'S MARRIAGE   Fiona Lowe
PROPOSAL

April

A BABY FOR EVE   Maggie Kingsley
MARRYING THE MILLIONAIRE DOCTOR   Alison Roberts
HIS VERY SPECIAL BRIDE   Joanna Neil
CITY SURGEON, OUTBACK BRIDE   Lucy Clark
A BOSS BEYOND COMPARE   Dianne Drake
THE EMERGENCY DOCTOR'S   Molly Evans
CHOSEN WIFE

May

DR DEVEREUX'S PROPOSAL   Margaret McDonagh
CHILDREN'S DOCTOR,   Meredith Webber
MEANT-TO-BE WIFE
ITALIAN DOCTOR, SLEIGH-BELL BRIDE   Sarah Morgan
CHRISTMAS AT WILLOWMERE   Abigail Gordon
DR ROMANO'S CHRISTMAS BABY   Amy Andrews
THE DESERT SURGEON'S SECRET SON   Olivia Gates

MILLS & BOON®
Pure reading pleasure™

0209 LP 2P P1 Medical

MEDICAL™

Large Print

June

A MUMMY FOR CHRISTMAS	Caroline Anderson
A BRIDE AND CHILD WORTH WAITING FOR	Marion Lennox
ONE MAGICAL CHRISTMAS	Carol Marinelli
THE GP'S MEANT-TO-BE BRIDE	Jennifer Taylor
THE ITALIAN SURGEON'S CHRISTMAS MIRACLE	Alison Roberts
CHILDREN'S DOCTOR, CHRISTMAS BRIDE	Lucy Clark

July

THE GREEK DOCTOR'S NEW-YEAR BABY	Kate Hardy
THE HEART SURGEON'S SECRET CHILD	Meredith Webber
THE MIDWIFE'S LITTLE MIRACLE	Fiona McArthur
THE SINGLE DAD'S NEW-YEAR BRIDE	Amy Andrews
THE WIFE HE'S BEEN WAITING FOR	Dianne Drake
POSH DOC CLAIMS HIS BRIDE	Anne Fraser

August

CHILDREN'S DOCTOR, SOCIETY BRIDE	Joanna Neil
THE HEART SURGEON'S BABY SURPRISE	Meredith Webber
A WIFE FOR THE BABY DOCTOR	Josie Metcalfe
THE ROYAL DOCTOR'S BRIDE	Jessica Matthews
OUTBACK DOCTOR, ENGLISH BRIDE	Leah Martyn
SURGEON BOSS, SURPRISE DAD	Janice Lynn

MILLS & BOON®
Pure reading pleasure™

0209 LP 2P P2 Medical